1866 - 1991

125th

ANNIVERSARY

DEATH KNELL

NICHOLAS WILDE

HENRY HOLT AND COMPANY ◆ NEW YORK

First American edition
Published by Henry Holt and Company, Inc.,
115 West 18th Street, New York, New York 10011.
Published simultaneously in Canada by Fitzhenry & Whiteside Ltd.,
195 Allstate Parkway, Markham, Ontario L3R 4T8.
Originally published in Great Britain by William Collins Sons & Co. Ltd, London.

Library of Congress Cataloging-in-Publication Data
Wilde, Nicholas.
Death knell / Nicholas Wilde.
Summary: Tim and Jamie investigate the unsolved murder of old
Mr. Jefford who was found with a smashed skull in the church crypt.
ISBN 0-8050-1851-4
[1. Mystery and detective stories. 2. Murder—Fiction.]
I. Title.
PZ7.W64582De 1991
[Fic]—dc20   91-19386

Henry Holt books are available at special discounts
for bulk purchases for sales promotions, premiums,
fund-raising, or educational use. Special editions
or book excerpts can also be created to specification.
Printed in the United States of America
on acid-free paper. ∞
1 3 5 7 9 10 8 6 4 2

DEATH KNELL

◆ ◆ ◆

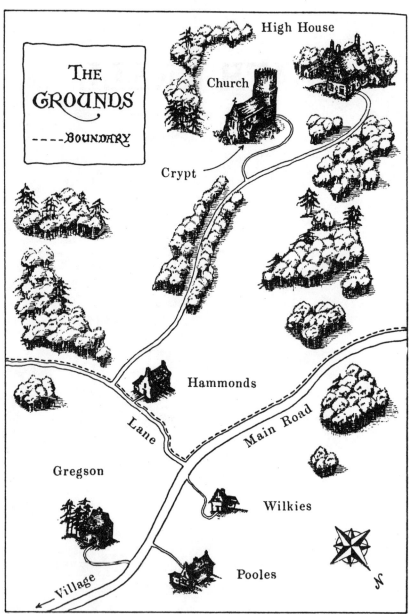

High House

THE
GROUNDS
----BOUNDARY

Church

Crypt

Hammonds

Lane

Main Road

Gregson

Wilkies

Pooles

Village

N

NW

PART I

—— ♦ ♦ ♦ ——

1

—— ◆ ——

Tim's voice fell to a whisper.

"D'you know what I reckon, Jamie? I reckon there was a death up there once. A nasty one. You can sort of feel it."

"Feel what?"

"I'm not sure, really. Just something creepy."

"Disused churches always feel like that."

"Not as much as that one. The whole place is as creepy as hell."

Jamie didn't answer for a moment. He looked across at Tim, but Tim was only shadow, knees drawn up to chin against the facing wall. Darkness had closed in around the cottage. January darkness. Too dark to go on sitting here, out in the hallway. They should put the lights on, go into the kitchen. But it had grown too dark to move.

"How many times have you been inside it, Tim? In the old church, I mean?"

"Only once. Grandad showed me round it about a year and a half ago."

"Is there anything in there? Any pews and stuff?"

"No, it's empty."

"That's probably what makes it creepy."

"It's not just that. I told you, it's got a sort of feeling about it. I bet I'm right, anyway."

"I reckon you just imagined it because of this old legend there's supposed to be about it."

"I didn't even know there *was* a legend then. I hadn't heard a word about it till Alex Jefford came out with it before the meeting tonight. And I still haven't got the foggiest what it's all about."

"Didn't your grandad mention it when he showed you round?"

"Hell, how many more times? I don't know any more about it than you do, OK?"

"Well, you've had enough vacations up here, haven't you? It seems weird your gran and grandad haven't let on to you about it."

"Like I said, it must be something pretty spooky, I suppose, or they would have. Gran's funny about stuff like that."

"I wouldn't have thought she's the sort who believes in ghosts. She doesn't, does she?"

"Search me. She always gets shifty when that kind of stuff crops up, that's all I know."

"What about your grandad?"

"Grandad? He's not exactly likely to *admit* it even if he does believe in them, is he?"

"Why not?"

"Because he's a vicar, cretin. Catch!"

Tim's shadow shifted and a little globe of light took shape within it, greenish white. Jamie tensed. It hovered for a moment, then clicked against the floor and sprang towards him. He caught it on the rebound and bounced it back. Tim's fingers quenched it.

"This ball's busted already."

"It's probably all that glow-in-the-dark stuff you put on it."

"It's pretty effective, though. Hey, Jamie, we could try a game later on if you like, when they've finished with the dining-room table. With all the lights off. Sort of phantom Ping-Pong."

The little phantom swooped again and leapt at Jamie's ear. He held it there a moment and listened to its hollow whisper when his finger stroked it. Then he flipped it back and watched it vanish. He turned his head. At the far end of the hallway the meeting in the dining room was still in progress. The voices rose and fell. Tim's gran and grandad. Alex Jefford from the High House. Other voices he couldn't be quite sure of, voices from the village. The sounds weren't words, just murmurs, like part of the stillness of the cottage. The door was firmly closed. At its foot, a crack of light made wrinkles in the flagstones.

"How long are they going to be in there, Tim?"

"Not long now. They'll be through at seven on the dot."

"You sure?"

"Course I'm sure. It's been the same every time I've been here. They start at six and go on for an hour, first Monday of every month. Then Gran and Grandad send them packing, except for Alex, and we chow down for a couple of hours before Old Jefford arrives for bridge or whatever they play. Things go like clockwork in villages, especially Norfolk ones. Same things same time every day. I always know what Gran and Grandad are doing up here in Lychwood, even when I'm back home in London."

"What do they find to talk about in these Church Committee meetings?"

"Beats me. I bet it's all pretty boring whatever it is."

"It's not anything to do with . . . with the old church up in the Grounds, is it?"

"Course it's not, dodo. They're people from Grandad's own church downtown."

"Who's in there? Have I met them round the village?"

"Not to talk to. There's only six, anyway. Apart from Gran and Grandad and Alex Jefford, there's just Mrs. Gregson and Doc Poole and Old Wilkie. We saw Gregson down in the grocer's the other day, remember?"

"Oh, her." Jamie remembered. An elderly, heavy-looking woman, dressed in black. "She looked a bit frosty."

"Oh, she's all right. Works up at the High House."

"What sort of work?"

"Every sort, as far as I can make out. Cleans and cooks for Old Jefford, that kind of stuff. Rather her than me, that's all I can say. And she's got Alex to cope with as well now, since he's come to live there. Old Jefford's his great-uncle."

"How long's he been there?"

"Alex? Oh, only a couple of years, since his job moved him up to Wells. It's pretty convenient for him, I suppose, but I still don't know how he does it. I'd rather ship out than cope with Old Jefford."

"Does Mrs. Gregson live with them?"

"Hell, no. She's no relation or anything. Hers is that hunky-looking place on the right on the way down to the village."

"She's pretty hunky herself."

"Not your type?"

"Funny."

"She wasn't Mr. Gregson's type either. He took a walk years ago."

"Where did he go to?"

"Haven't a clue. Just up and left, I think. Hasn't been seen since."

"And who's Doc Poole?"

"Local GP. Lives down a bit from Mrs. Gregson, over on the other side of the road."

"The bony old bloke? What's he like?"

"Pretty deadly. Mrs. Poole's OK, though."

"Is he the only doc round here?"

"Course he is. It's not London."

"Your gran and grandad use him, then?"

"Course. Everybody does. Except for Old Jefford, that is. He goes to some private doc in Norwich."

"Why?"

"Give me a break, Jamie, this isn't Trivial Pursuit. How am I supposed to know?"

"You know one hell of a lot for somebody who only comes here twice a year."

"That's villages for you. Gossip's the only hobby they've got up here. You can get the low-down on everything—except the really juicy stuff, that is."

"Like what?"

"Like legends."

"Oh."

"And speaking of ghosts—there's one in the dining room right now."

"What?" Jamie glanced back towards the crack of light beneath the doorway. In spite of himself, he felt a shiver walk along his spine. "What're you talking about?"

"Old Wilkie. Even more ancient than Old Jefford, I should think."

"Have I seen him?"

"Doubt it. He's only about four foot high. Talk about weird."

"Why's he on the Committee, then?"

"Probably just because he's always been on it—I reckon he was here before the village was. He even gives Grandad the creeps sometimes. His is that little cottage opposite the end of our lane."

"The ramshackle one?"

"That's it. Joe's all right, though."

"Joe?"

"His son. You've seen him—old blue van. Does odd jobs round the village, delivering groceries and doing gardening, stuff like that. He's a genius compared with Old Wilkie."

"Is there a Mrs. Wilkie?"

"No, and I'm not exactly surprised, either. Who'd want to shack up with him? Joe still does, though—live with his dad, I mean. Yuk." Tim's voice sank again, to a dark whisper. "You know something? If there does turn out to be a ghost in this legend, I bet it'll be Old Wilkie."

"Cretin." A thin blade of cold knifed its way along the flagstones. Jamie drew his heels in closer. "Doesn't sound to me as if they're running out of things to talk about in there. Sounds as if they're in there for the night."

"Don't panic. Seven on the dot Grandad'll chuck them out. He always does. He hates Church Committee meetings."

"Does he?" Jamie smiled. "He's something really different, isn't he?"

"Different from what?"

"From what I expected. From normal vicars."

"I wouldn't have thought you knew any vicars."

"I've seen some on TV, haven't I?"

"Oh brilliant. World expert, then."

"I was nervous about meeting him last week."

"You could've fooled me. You'd been hinting for an invite up here for long enough."

"Only because you couldn't wait to get back up here every holiday, that's all. I wanted to see what the big attraction was."

"Found out, have you?"

"I reckon."

"Go on, then. What?"

Jamie paused. He frowned slightly in the darkness. "Well . . . there's your gran and grandad, isn't there? They're great. And the village and everything. And . . . well, something about Norfolk, I suppose."

"Such as?"

"I . . . I'm not sure. It's so different up here somehow, that's all. It's going to be weird going back home to London tomorrow, back to school and all that kind of stuff. I can't explain, really. It's just that Norfolk's so sort of . . . well, *old*."

His gaze drifted with his thoughts, to where the front door of the cottage hid in shadow; then through it, to the dark that lay outside. Yes, Norfolk was old, far older than London. Darker. More secret. Full of old, dark secrets.

"Catch!"

Jamie jumped, snatching at the ball that leapt towards him. It scuttled off and vanished, up along the hall.

"Klutz!"

"I wasn't ready, that's all. I was thinking . . . Tim, you know this cottage is the vicarage of Lychwood—"

"I'd just about figured that out, thanks."

"Well, how come it's stuck up here inside the grounds of the High House, when your grandad's church is right down in the middle of the village? D'you reckon it used to be the vicarage of the other church? The disused one up in the Grounds, I mean?"

"Might've been, I suppose. Doubt it, though. This place isn't half as old as the old church. It used to be the gate house of the Grounds, that's all. That's why it's called the Lodge Cottage. The driveway outside goes on for miles—

well, half a mile anyway—right up through the trees to the High House."

Jamie saw it in his mind's eye, the view that he and Tim had from the window of their bedroom. Tim had pointed out the chimneys of the High House where Alex Jefford lived with his great-uncle, up beyond the avenue of beeches. And between the High House and the gateway was the tower of the church . . .

"So apart from this cottage, it all belongs to Old Jefford, does it? The Grounds and the High House and everything?"

"The whole works. Sick, isn't it?"

"What about the old church? Is that his as well?"

"I'm not sure, really. It's on his land."

"But your gran and grandad look after it, don't they?"

"Well, sort of. Grandad keeps the keys down here in the cottage and goes and opens up if any tourists want a look at it. But that's in summer mostly and there aren't many even then. Lychwood's a bit off the track for tourists. And Gran just goes up on Monday mornings for a quick clean-round."

"Every Monday?"

"You bet. Clockwork, like I said. That's where she was this morning."

"There can't be much to clean up if it's empty, can there?"

"Loads, she says. Bat droppings mainly."

"You kidding?"

"Course I'm not kidding. Hell, you don't believe a word I say, do you? There're thousands of the things up there, up in the beams."

"Why doesn't Old Jefford keep the keys and see to it himself?"

"What a laugh. He hates people, that's why. And he's too ancient, anyway."

"What's he like?"

"I just told you. Gruesome. About five hundred years old and stone-deaf. You'll see for yourself at nine o'clock, anyhow, when he comes down for bridge. It's his one big outing of the week."

"What does he do all the rest of the time?"

"God knows. Just slogs away at his book, I should think, some sort of history of the village he's writing. He's been at it for years. It's real high-brow, Grandad says."

"Your grandad's read it, then?"

"Bits of it. Old Jefford talks it over with him and Gran on Mondays sometimes. They're about the only people he does talk to round here—he's not exactly the most popular bloke in Lychwood. I usually make myself pretty scarce when he's around, but tonight's going to be the big exception."

"How d'you mean?"

"Hell, Jamie, you're so thick it's untrue. The legend, dodo. The thing you've been on about for the last half hour, remember?"

"OK, OK. But what's the link-up with Old Jefford?"

"From what Alex told Grandad before the meeting, we're going to be in luck. He said Old Jefford's busting with some new discovery he's made about it for this book of his and he wants to give Grandad the dope on it when he comes down after supper. So we've got to make sure we're in on it. And even Gran's not going to stop us this time, ghosts or no ghosts."

Jamie didn't answer. Another shiver touched him. Tim's shadow hugged itself. His voice continued from the darkness.

"Tonight's the night, Jamie. The legend of the old church.

And I'm right—you'll see. There was death mixed up in it somewhere, as sure as bloody sure."

The meeting was over.

At the front end of the cottage the voices had grown loud now, become words again. The dining-room door had opened. Light flooded out.

Tim's gran, Mrs. Hammond, paused for a moment, silhouetted in the doorway, then came quickly down the hall towards the kitchen. She stopped before she reached it.

"What on earth are you two doing sitting out here in the dark? You must be frozen. Why didn't you go into the sitting room? There's a fire in there."

"Hi, Gran. We were just keeping guard while you all had your séance."

"Shush, Tim, they'll hear you. You shouldn't call it that."

"Grandad does."

"Not when there're people around. You can come and give me a hand with the supper in a minute. We'll eat in the sitting room, I think. It'll be warmer."

She stepped between the boys, on into the kitchen, as another, larger figure came out into the hall. Mrs. Gregson. Tim and Jamie watched her. Her back was turned towards them as she reached up to the coatstand. The coat came free, a bulk of blackness. She shrugged her own dark bulk inside it, and the front door closed behind her. A moment later Dr. Poole followed, as dry and bony as Jamie had remembered. Then he too vanished. Neither he nor Mrs. Gregson had seen that they'd been watched.

For some odd reason which he couldn't quite decipher, Jamie felt increasingly uneasy. Perhaps all the talking in the darkness . . . Or the feeling that he'd somehow just been spying . . . He found himself looking at his watch. It was 7:02 exactly. So Tim was right in his prediction that— His thought remained unfinished. Someone else had just come out into the hallway . . .

Jamie stared, not breathing. The little figure watched him, standing there, unmoving. Unmoving, except for the head. The head was wagging; the old face rose and fell, one eye screwed up, the mouth lopsided, as if it might be smiling. A smile that seemed to know things . . . then the silent watching ended. The figure turned and left them. The front door closed again.

Tim raised his eyebrows, grinning.

"See what I mean?"

"Was that—?"

"Old Wilkie. He's completely gaga."

"Perhaps . . . perhaps he was just trying to be friendly or something."

"No way of knowing. Anyway, I told you he'd scare you."

"Who said he scared me?"

"Oh come off it, you should see your face. So admit it."

"OK, so he scared me. Big deal."

Tim's laughter was cut short. The dining-room door had opened again. Familiar faces this time, and the last of the Committee. Alex Jefford and Tim's grandad.

It was the vicar who saw them first.

"Hello, you two—séance over, you'll be glad to hear. What are you doing down there? Cooling your bottoms?"

"Gran said we weren't to use that word."

"What word? Bottoms?"

"No, dodo. Séance."

"Did she? Oh well, I expect she's right. Go and fetch yourself a drink, Alex, then we'll have another quick look through these notes before supper. The whiskey's on the bookcase in the sitting room."

"Thanks, I need it."

The vicar stepped back inside the dining room as Alex came on down along the hall. Then Tim yelled out.

"Hey, watch it, Alex! Mind the phantom!"

Jamie jumped as violently as Alex. For an instant, Alex froze.

"By your foot—you nearly stepped on it."

Alex drew a breath. He stooped and gathered up the table-tennis ball.

"Is this your phantom?"

"That's the one."

"Catch, then."

He threw the ball to Tim and came on down towards them. As he passed, Tim sprang up as if on impulse and caught him by the sleeve. He glanced along the hall and dropped his voice.

"Alex—speaking of phantoms . . . I heard what you said to Grandad earlier. Or a bit of it. About Mr. Jefford and things, and this new discovery he's made about—"

Mrs. Hammond's voice called from the kitchen.

"Tim! Come on, please."

"OK, Gran, coming . . . About this sort of legend there's supposed to be. You know, the old church . . . " He faltered, looking helplessly between Alex and the kitchen door. "Well . . . d'you reckon me and Jamie can be in on it?"

"In on it?"

"We sort of thought it'd give us a chance of finding out what the legend's all about."

"You mean your gran and grandad haven't told you?"

"Not a word."

Alex paused for a moment, then he smiled. "Oh, I'm sure

we can soon fix that. If you're really keen to hear it, I don't see why you've got to wait till Uncle arrives."

"What? D'you mean you'll tell us?"

"Well, not out here." He winked. "I think later might be better, don't you? How about after supper? Yes, you just mention it straight after supper. Ghost stories are for round the fire."

He winked again, and moved off down the hall.

Tim swung back round to Jamie with a grin of triumph. And Jamie responded. But only with an effort. He felt suddenly, irrationally, afraid.

2

———◆———

"**A**lex, do you really think you should?"

"Oh come on, Mrs. Hammond, they're fourteen, aren't they? And I bet they've heard worse things than this at school."

"But it's all such silly rubbish."

"All the less harm in telling them, then."

Mrs. Hammond set her empty plate down in the hearth. She hesitated, and glanced towards her husband.

"What do you think, David?"

The vicar hesitated too. For a few seconds he stared at the fire. Then he raised his head and shrugged.

"Oh I expect Alex is right, Joyce. The worst it can do is to give them one sleepless night. They'll be back home tomorrow." He turned to face them. "But *I* don't intend to have a sleepless night, so don't come waking *me* up if you get the heebie-jeebies."

Tim grinned. "Oh come off it, Grandad. Anyway, it'd *better* be pretty creepy after all this build-up."

"It is."

Mr. Hammond's voice had changed; its smile had left it. In the silence which followed his reply, the fire crackled loudly.

Mrs. Hammond was the first to move. She stood up and shook her apron.

"Well, I'm not going to waste time listening to that stuff and nonsense all over again."

She gathered up the plates and dishes and clattered them in piles on a tray. Jamie was reminded of something he'd once read, an old superstition. Noise was supposed to ward off evil spirits. He wondered for a moment if she was doing it on purpose.

"Open the door for me, Tim, will you? I can manage after that. I'm going to get the washing-up done before Mr. Jefford arrives."

She left the room without looking back.

When Tim had closed the door behind her, Mr. Hammond shifted a little in his chair and poked thoughtfully at the fire.

"Have you any idea what your great-uncle *has* found out, Alex?"

"None at all, apart from what I told you earlier. He seemed pretty excited about it though, whatever it was. His book's the only thing he ever thinks about these days, so if he *has* got hold of something new for it he won't rest till he gets to the bottom of every last detail. All I could gather is that he's got some new angle on the church from somebody."

"But you're sure it's about the legend?"

"Oh yes, there's no doubt about that, from what he said."

Mr. Hammond frowned slightly. "It seems odd that anything new should come to light after all this time. And he didn't give you any hint about what this information might be?"

"Not a word. But you know what he's like—won't let on about anything until he wants to, especially to me. He's definitely intending to let you in on it this evening, though. Apparently he'll be certain of his facts by then."

"How do you mean?"

"He didn't say much more than that. Just that he was hoping for a meeting which would settle it one way or the other."

"A meeting? When?"

"Before he comes down here, presumably. But don't ask me who with—as I said, he's not exactly generous with his information where I'm concerned. And I only saw him for a few minutes over tea anyway, before I came down here for our pre-Committee session. Mrs. Gregson stayed on for a bit to clear away the tea-things, but she said nobody had called by the time she left at five forty-five." He glanced at his watch and then across at Tim and Jamie. "Anyway, it's nearly quarter to eight already, so we'd better get on with this tale if we're going to and put these poor lads out of their misery. Are you going to tell it, or shall I?"

Mr. Hammond looked suddenly over to the sofa as if he'd forgotten for a moment that the boys were there.

"I suppose I'd better," he said. "You can chime in if you know more of the details than I do, Alex."

"I doubt that. I'll probably learn a thing or two myself."

"Well, for what it's worth then . . . "

He drew a long breath.

"I suppose you could say that Henry VIII started the whole wretched business. Four hundred and fifty years ago. Our present church down in the village hadn't been built then, so the church up in the Grounds was the only one in Lychwood. It had its own priest, of course, and had probably been in pretty full use for a couple of centuries. Until, that is, old Henry came along and put a stop to it. That was the time of the Dissolution of the Monasteries.

"Well, the church met the same fate as hundreds of others. It was closed down as a place of the old Catholic worship, and the priest was told to pack his bags and go. He didn't go at once, though—not for some weeks, it appears. And it was during those weeks that the . . . the strangeness is said to have begun."

"The strangeness, Grandad? What strangeness?"

"Something happened up there. Or is supposed to have happened. And the story of it spread through the village like the plague. They were superstitious times, of course, and the tale probably grew in the telling—there are hundreds of old wives' tales that must have started like that. But there's something that makes this story different, something you don't usually find. It hasn't come down to us only by word of mouth, you see. It was recorded in writing, at the very time it was happening."

"In writing? Where?"

"You can read it yourself if you want to, in the Norfolk Archives Office in Norwich. It's the old priest's daybook."

"Daybook?"

"A sort of record he'd kept—official stuff mainly, about baptisms and the like—right through his time here in Lychwood until the church was closed. He records the date of the closing exactly. But, after that, when you'd expect the daybook to finish, it doesn't. There are another three short entries. The first one's dated the evening of the day the church closed."

He fell silent for a moment, frowning at the fire, as if reading the old words again in the flames. But it was Alex who spoke them.

"God has departed from His house, but where God is not, there shall another power enter in and take possession."

He spoke them softly. In spite of the flames, a coldness crept up Jamie's back.

Mr. Hammond drew closer to the fire.

"Yes," he said. "Yes. Another power."

"What power, Grandad?"

Mr. Hammond didn't answer. He went on as if to himself.

"The second entry comes later, undated like the third. But there must be a few days gap between them. They're both very strange. *Already has . . .* "

He frowned again, trying to remember. In the stillness Alex's voice returned.

"Already has his creature come forth from his hiding in the earth. I have felt his presence here. I have seen him."

He paused. The sofa cushions stirred as Tim sat slightly forward. Then Alex began again, more softly than before. And Jamie knew that this was the third and final entry before the daybook closed in silence.

"This day have we taken the bell from its place in the tower, that it ring no more. And the earth where he hides have we sealed with the stone, that he be hidden from us forever."

Only the fire moved now. It sank a little, and a tiny wraith of smoke slid out across the room.

"But . . . but what does it mean, Grandad? The bell's still there, isn't it?"

"Oh, it's back there now."

"But the rest of it—I mean, what stone's he talking about? Is there any way of knowing?"

"Oh yes. You've seen it yourself."

"I've seen it?"

"You asked me about it a couple of years ago, when I showed you round."

"Not the . . . " Tim started suddenly, drawing their eyes

to him. "It's the one in the floor of the crypt, isn't it? The one right in the middle! It is, isn't it, Grandad?"

Mr. Hammond hesitated for a second, as if unwilling to go on. "Yes. Yes, that's the one."

Jamie heard his own voice now, oddly quiet.

"The crypt, Tim? What's the crypt?"

Tim described it, breathless. And in his mind's eye Jamie saw what he described. He saw the little chapel with its single narrow window, built out from the north wall of the church. Not a proper crypt at all, but referred to as the crypt for as long as local people could remember. Perhaps because its floor was so much lower than the level of the church. He saw the flight of steps that led him downward, starting from the door inside the nave, and the rough flint floor that met him where they ended. And in the middle of the floor he saw the stone. It looked strange there. Senseless. Like an old, forgotten tombstone, set flat into the earth.

Tim's voice was still speaking. But not to Jamie now.

"The legend, Grandad. Will you tell us? From beginning to end?"

"The legend. Yes. It begins in the church, and ends there. In a church as locked and empty as it is tonight. That was the strangeness."

"What was? What happened?"

"Something that couldn't happen. Not in a locked and empty church. It was the bell, you see. It rang."

"But—"

"It rang one single stroke, and the squire in the High House heard it. And he was the only one who had the key. He'd locked the church himself, that night."

"What . . . what did he do?"

"The only thing he could do. He took the key and a

candle, and went out. Expecting, perhaps, to find the place broken into and the practical joker still inside. But he didn't. He found it exactly as he'd left it, locked and in darkness. So he opened the door and went in.

"The candle flame didn't carry far, but far enough at least to show him that he hadn't been mistaken. A few feet from where he stood inside the doorway, the light fell on the bell rope. It was still swinging.

"He went on into the church. At first, he wasn't sure what it was that caught his eye. But he *was* sure that someone, or something, had moved. He called out but no one answered. So he crept on again, up the nave. And it was then that he was certain that he saw it."

Their question hung in the air, unspoken. The vicar went on, as if in answer.

"A figure. Or the shadow of a figure, ahead of him, edging away. He followed, until he saw it slip out of sight. But he was sure about the doorway it had gone through: the only possible doorway, the one leading down into the crypt. He knew now that he had it. It was cornered. From the crypt there was no way out. It was only when he reached the place himself that his fear really started. He remembered then, you see. The crypt was always kept locked—the key to it was up at the House. And without it, not a soul could get inside. He glanced around again, but the church was hushed and empty, so he summoned all his courage and tried the handle. It was as he'd feared it would be. The door was still as it always was. It was locked.

"But even that wasn't the worst. When he got back to the House he found everyone in chaos. Something terrible had happened. It was one of his old servants. He was dead."

"*Dead*? But . . . how?"

"Oh, natural causes, and nothing suspicious. Except for just one thing, perhaps. And that one thing alarmed him more than all the rest. You see, the death had been so sudden, without any kind of warning. And it had come on the stroke of the bell."

Mr. Hammond stopped speaking. Faintly, in the kitchen, crockery tinkled. Tim's voice was a whisper.

"But it could've been coincidence, couldn't it? Couldn't it, Grandad?"

"Yes. That time it could. And the second time perhaps. But the third time? The fourth?"

"The *fourth*?"

"Four times. Four deaths in the village, and always the same single stroke of the bell in a church that was locked and deserted. And nothing to show what had rung it, until . . . "

"Until what?"

"Until it happened again. The villagers were ready for it this time, went straight to the church with the squire and the priest. And there was little doubting now. Whoever it was, whatever it was, they swore they saw it, edging away as the squire had described. And, just as before, it slipped out of sight by the door to the crypt. But this time the squire had brought the key.

"When the door was unlocked and pushed open, they lifted their candles and looked in. There was just light enough to pick out something in the shadows down below. Unclearly, perhaps, but they saw it. And they hadn't expected what they saw. Whatever they had followed was crouched down low now, right in the middle of the floor. And it seemed somehow to be . . . to be burrowing. Strangely and horribly, down into the earth. And then it vanished."

He was silent. Jamie felt too cold now, for speaking. It was Tim who spoke the question for them both.

"What was it, Grandad? Did they see what it was? Perhaps it was an animal . . . It must've been, mustn't it?"

Mr. Hammond glanced away from the fireplace, round towards the sofa, and slowly eyed the two of them in turn.

"Perhaps. Yes. Perhaps that was it. Just an animal."

It was Alex who answered.

"Why not tell them, Mr. Hammond? Tell them the ending."

Jamie waited, dreading what was coming, not knowing what he dreaded.

The vicar shrugged. "Well, they went on down the steps to the place where they'd seen it disappear, and . . . oh, they were probably mistaken about what they thought they saw there. It was strange though, all the same. It had left no trace, you see, no evidence behind it. The earth was still untouched."

For a moment, there was silence. Then Mr. Hammond sat back in his armchair. "So there you are," he said. "That's the Lychwood legend for you. You know the rest, you've heard it from the old priest's daybook. The bell was taken down. And the middle of the floor was sealed tightly with the stone. *That he be hidden from us forever.*" He smiled. "It seems to have worked, too. Whatever it was, it's never come back."

With a suddenness which made them start, the clock on the mantelpiece began its chime of eight. Mr. Hammond smiled again.

"Well, I warned you. So, what do you think? Was it creepy enough for you?"

But his question was never to be answered.

As the clock died into silence, another sound came. Faint at first, and distant, as unreal as an echo. Like an echo of the final chime. But it wasn't an echo. It came from outside, from the darkness. They knew what they were hearing.

The church bell had tolled one single stroke.

3

$\diamond$

A crash came from the kitchen. A plate rolled and spun, faster and faster, spiraling itself into the floor. Then there was silence.

Mr. Hammond moved first. He left the room and dashed across the hallway. Tim and Jamie listened, frozen to the sofa. Faintly, they heard Mrs. Hammond speaking.

"It's all right. An accident, that's all. It's just that I thought . . . I thought I heard—"

"Don't worry, Joyce. It's nothing, I'm sure."

"But when I came away this morning I locked—"

"It was only the wind."

"David, there isn't a breath of—"

"Please, Joyce. It's all right. You get this mess cleared up and I'll be back before you've finished."

"Back?"

"I'll go and see. Make sure."

"David—"

"Come on now—the boys . . . "

He didn't say the rest. Perhaps his face had said it for him. When Mrs. Hammond answered, her voice was firm again and loud.

"Yes. Yes, of course. You'll be back by twenty past or so

if you go now, and I'll have the kettle boiled by then for another cup of tea. It's freezing outside."

Alex was on his feet now. He moved quicky out into the hall. There was a soft exchange of voices, then the vicar reappeared.

"Well, you two, at least that's blown our old story wide open—coincidences do happen after all, you see? And you can imagine what they'd have spun out of this one in the old days." He laughed, but his face was pale. "I'm just popping up there with Alex. It's pointless of course, but it'll put your gran's mind at rest."

The sofa shifted suddenly as Tim leapt up.

"OK. We'll come with you."

"No, Tim, I'd rather—"

"Oh come on, Grandad, why not? You said there's nothing to be scared of, didn't you?" He laughed too, as Mr. Hammond had a moment before. Jamie watched him. The same laughter, in a face of ashen white. "You don't seriously reckon there *could* be anything up there, do you?"

"No, of course not—"

"Well, that's OK then, isn't it?"

"Look, Tim. I'd rather you stayed here, that's all. With your gran."

"Why? Hey, she's not scared, is she?"

"No, it's not like that at all. It's just . . . "

He hesitated, fumbling for an answer to Tim's challenge. Alex broke the tension, stepping swiftly back inside the doorway, pulling on his overcoat and gloves. He winked at Tim across the vicar's shoulder, but his voice was urgent.

"Oh let them come if they want to, Mr. Hammond. We really ought to be moving."

Tim didn't wait to hear the answer. He left the room and ran towards the stairs.

"Come on, Jamie!"

Jamie followed. He slipped numbly between Alex and the vicar, out into the hall. Mrs. Hammond was standing in the entrance to the kitchen. She didn't speak or move but her eyes were on him, pleading with him not to go. For an instant he faltered. Then he raced on past her, up the stairs.

After the warmth and brightness of the fireside, the landing was sharp with sudden cold. Mrs. Hammond had been right, it was freezing outside. Tim was in their bedroom, floundering his way into a second sweater. His face burst out into the open, pale and grinning.

"Get a move on, Jamie."

"OK, give me a chance." Muffled in parka and sweaters, he struggled with his boots. He spoke, not looking up. "Hey, Tim, d'you reckon the rest of the village heard it?"

"I doubt it, they've probably all got their TVs on by now. We're a good bit nearer than they are anyway."

"What about the High House? That's nearer than we are, isn't it? Old Jefford must've heard it."

"You're joking. I told you, he's pretty well stone-deaf. He can barely hear his own doorbell."

"But if this visitor he's supposed to be having's still there . . . "

"Oh come *on*, Jamie, we'll find out soon enough. It makes no difference one way or the other. Look, I'm heading on down. We don't want to give Grandad time to change his mind about us going. So step on it, OK?"

He left the room. His footsteps thudded down the stairs and Jamie was alone.

He moved towards the window for his scarf. The curtains were undrawn and the tiny leaded panes were blind and black. He paused, looking at them, screwing up his eyes in an effort to see out. He knew what they'd have shown him in daylight. The avenue of beech trees rising slowly upward and ending at the chimneys of the High House and the tower of the church. But now they showed him nothing but the night. He'd be out there soon . . . He felt suddenly frightened. He shouldn't go out there tonight, none of them should. He dragged the curtains shut and ran downstairs.

On the bottom step, he halted.

There was silence in the hallway. He saw the little group that had assembled there. He looked from one to the other. Mrs. Hammond hadn't moved. She was standing where he'd left her, in the doorway to the kitchen. A few feet farther on, wrapped against the cold that was to come, Tim stood side by side with Alex. In the entrance to the dining room, the vicar faced them. He looked bewildered, as if waiting for an answer. None came. He spoke abruptly, the same question he must have asked before.

"Are you sure, Joyce?"

"I've told you I am."

"Are you sure you put them back when you came in before lunch?"

"David, you know I did. You were in the dining room yourself. You saw me. I put them back inside the cupboard."

"Well they're not there now. Keys can't just disappear."

"Perhaps somebody's taken them—"

"But why on earth should anybody want to? Nobody *could* have taken them, for goodness sake. Nobody knows where they're kept, except for the Committee."

The silence came again, tenser than before, as if the final words had told them something that shouldn't have been spoken. Mr. Hammond turned to Tim.

"Tim, have *you* taken them?"

"No, Grandad, of course I haven't. What would I—"

Suddenly the frozen grouping broke. Alex strode forward to the outer door.

"Come on, it's five past eight already. We'd better go and find out who the hell's playing about up there."

With a rattle, the front door was pulled open. Jamie felt a rush of icy air sweep down the hallway. The night was coming in. He left the stairs and followed, out into the porch. Mrs. Hammond's footsteps came behind him. Her voice faltered out a final plea.

"David, wait a minute. Whatever it is up there . . . "

"It'll be all right, Joyce."

It was too late. The vicar swung the door towards him, slamming out her words. Whatever it was up there, it had begun now. There could be no going back.

They went as quickly as they could through the still darkness, two abreast along the avenue of trees. In the whole vast night there was no movement but their own. Earth and sky were locked together in the grip of frost. Jamie felt its touch against his cheeks, a scorch of cold black fire. It took his breath away. Tim stumbled on beside him across the frozen gravel. Ahead of them, where Alex and the vicar led the way with torches, the tiny rings of brightness made the night seem darker. When Mr. Hammond spoke, his words dissolved to vapor and drifted out behind him like a slipstream trail.

"It's too treacherous for your uncle to come down here on his own on a night like this, Alex."

"You try telling him. I offered to walk up at nine and get the car out, but you know his views on motoring. He says he prefers to use his legs."

"Surely he could give our bridge game a miss for this once."

"Break his routine? You'll be lucky. Look, when we've sorted out this other nonsense we could always step across to the House and have a word with him. He never leaves till quarter to nine so it gives us plenty of time."

"What's the time now?"

The pool of light in front of Alex sprang back towards his wrist.

"Eleven minutes past."

"Fine. If he still insists on coming, at least we could walk back down together."

For another two minutes they pressed along in silence. Then Alex paused and turned.

"Watch out for your ankles, you two. The path goes left out of the trees soon but it's pretty churned up round here."

They went in single file now. The avenue had narrowed. Wheel-ruts, mud-soft in summer, had set and hardened. Jamie began to pick his way across them. They looked yellow in the torchbeams, and bony as a rib cage. He faltered and hung back. A moment later the torchbeams, and Tim, had left him.

For an instant there was nothing but the soundless blackness. Then ahead, to the left, a voice rang out. It was Mr. Hammond's.

"What the hell—"

He stumbled on towards it. The lights returned, and the silhouetted figures. And beyond them another light, a tiny pointed beacon in a wall of night. The avenue had ended. Against the darkness of the sky a deeper darkness faced them. The nave and the tower of the church. Just as he'd seen them from his bedroom, only bigger now, more massive. And halfway down the nave-wall, projecting out towards them with its single little window, was the chapel that he'd heard about tonight. He knew it at once. It drew the eye towards it even though the shadows there were thickest. It was easy to see why.

"There's a light in there! In the crypt! There's someone in the crypt!"

The vicar didn't wait for any answer. With the others close behind him, he plunged into the gloom around the tower. They came to a halt at the western door. It was open.

"Keep with me. And mind the step."

His torchlight lengthened, swept straight ahead into the void, swung a little, leapt back at them again from the archway to the nave. He reached forward and clicked a switch. Deep inside the church a lightbulb blinked awake. Pillars struggled out of shadow.

Jamie stood with the others in the archway, looking. One night long ago, the squire had stood here too and looked about him as they were looking now. And seen . . . he shivered, thrusting the memory from him. The church was bare. No pews, or pulpit. And where the altar had once stood, there was only emptiness. There couldn't be anyone hiding here, not in the nave. There was nowhere to hide in here. He looked at the pillars, and up into the darkness of the beams. A movement caught his eye, like a tiny rag of night blown free. It snagged against a beam and hung there. Then another. And again. A shudder seized him. The whole place was crawling with bats.

Mr. Hammond turned to Alex, his voice low. "We'd better go and have a look at the crypt."

"The light's gone now, hasn't it?"

"Not necessarily. Not if they've got the door shut."

He was already stepping swiftly down the nave, Alex and Tim behind him. Jamie followed as if in a dream. The church closed round him. It smelt of cold wood, cold stone. And just beyond the smell of coldness, sickly sweet, a faint breath of corruption.

They'd stopped. Arrived. The door looked heavy, thick with wood and iron. From the keyhole, an eye-beam of light watched them. The vicar stooped down, straightened again, shook his head. His voice was a whisper.

"There's no key in there."

His hand reached out, took hold, eased gently upward. The door held firm. His quietness and caution left him. He was shouting now, wrenching the great metal ring of the handle, over and over. Inside, the latch was jerking, clacking up and down in the hollowness beyond. And Alex was beside him, his palm pounding against wood, a drumbeat in the silence. Then only echoes. The men fell back, helpless.

"There's something wrong in there, I know there is."

Alex's face tightened.

"Isn't there any other way into this place?"

"Come on, let's get round to the window. It's too small to get through but it's the only way of seeing what's going on in there."

"We'll never see through that, it's got glass an inch thick. And it doesn't open, does it?"

"We'll smash it."

They dashed back the way they'd come. The frost met them again, biting their faces. Outside the chapel now. In all the darkness, only the little window seemed alive.

"Find something. Anything. A stone . . . "

There was a sickening crash of stone on glass and lead. Bound in a scarf, shoulder-high, the vicar's hand struck again and again. The lattice of lead gave way. Panes flew inward and splintered into echoes far below. Then an arm of light thrust out into the night.

For a moment it shone clear. Then the vicar's head quenched it. They watched him, saw his rigid stillness. He staggered back. Alex stared at him, not moving, then lurched towards the gaping light.

"Alex, don't—"

But it was too late. Alex was there already, shaking off the hand which tried to stop him. At the window now, his head forced in against the brightness, his shoulders braced against the narrow cleft of stone. The silent stillness came again. So silent that they heard the tiny rasp and spasm of the leather as his fingers tightened on the outside wall. His voice broke from him. A single word, muffled at first and hollow, then shrieking outward like a cry of pain.

"Uncle!"

He'd turned now. The shaft of light leapt free. Only his face showed clearly, a crazy mask of whiteness suspended in the night.

"The door . . . We've got to get in there, for God's sake! We've got to get it open!"

Then both the men had vanished and the boys were left alone.

4

———◆———

Tim dropped back from the window. He turned away from Jamie, supporting his shoulder on the chapel wall. He didn't speak, or need to.

The cold sharpened. Jamie couldn't feel his legs now, only their trembling. But he knew that they were moving, closer to the light. He had no power to stop them. Stone reached out and touched him, on his fingers and his chest. The window edged forward, narrow as a halter, chafing his ears as it passed across them. Then it bit into his shoulders and his head was in the void.

His eyes stared downward, showing things to him, things he didn't want to see.

He was looking down into a bare unpillared chamber, through its single little window set high up in the wall. The floor lay fifteen feet below him. The door was eight feet from the ground in the farther corner, sideways to the window, on his left. Ten steps led down along the wall that faced him: a solid mass of stone set fast into the angle, like an outcrop of the wall itself. He could see them clearly, sharp and white with light. He knew now where the light came from, he could hear its tiny hissing. But it was a crazy thing to find in a place like this. A modern little camp-light

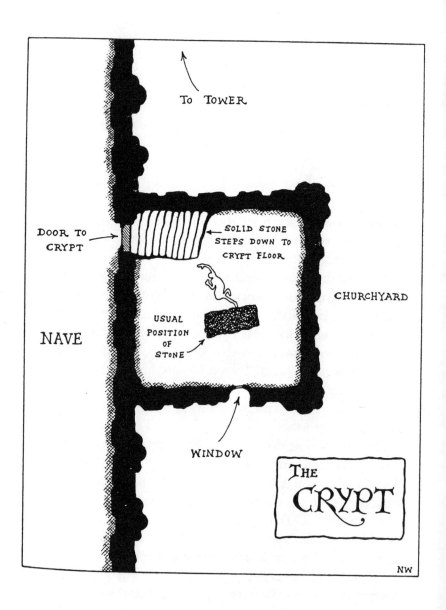

TO TOWER

DOOR TO
CRYPT

SOLID STONE
STEPS DOWN TO
CRYPT FLOOR

CHURCHYARD

USUAL
POSITION
OF
STONE

NAVE

WINDOW

THE
CRYPT

NW

with its cylinder of gas. And there could be no mistaking what it showed him.

A pickaxe lay abandoned in the middle of the chapel, and a small black iron shovel. Beside them, in the floor, a rectangle of earth showed like a six-foot gash of darkness. The soil was still untouched, still as blind as when the stone had lain across it and sealed it from the light. But now the stone had gone.

He raised his eyes, back towards the corner.

The stone. It was there, on the third step from the top. He could see its thickness from the window. Two inches, perhaps three. Like a buttress of granite, tipped at an angle, with its upper edge hard against the door.

He forced his eyes back down towards the floor . . .

The body was chest down, feet towards the window, a dark brown huddle of overcoat and scarf. One leg was drawn up, the other trailing limply, its shoe almost brushing the rectangle of earth. The arm was outstretched, the hand towards the steps, gloved, palm downward, in the pool of its own shadow like a small black crab. Just beyond the reach of the sprawling fingers was a bunch of keys.

He tore his eyes from it, staring wildly round the chapel. But there was nothing else to see here, not a single place where anything could hide.

A crash thundered out, deafening the silence. Then a touch against his shoulder made him cry aloud. He thrust himself backwards out into the night.

Tim was beside him.

"Come on, Jamie, they're trying to smash the door in."

"Who's in there, Tim?"

"Old Jefford by the look of it."

"What's happened to him? What's he doing in there?"

"God knows. Come on."

A second crash met them as they ran along the nave towards the doorway. Alex and the vicar reeled backwards in the shadows as if the noise itself had jolted them away.

"Again!"

The figures leapt again in a sickening collision of shoulders against wood and were flung back by the impact.

"Again!"

The volleys died away in echoes. The men fell back, bent double, breathing hard.

"We'll never shift it like this, Alex."

"We've got to! We can't just leave him in there!"

"There's iron an inch thick in that lock. I've—"

"We'll have to shift it on the hinge-side! We need a lever. A crowbar. Anything. And we've got to have a *doctor*!"

Tim broke from Jamie's side.

"We'll go, Alex. Me and Jamie can run over to the House. We'll phone Doc Poole."

"I wish to God you could, Tim. But there's no phone there. He wouldn't have one. Not with his deafness."

His voice choked. Mr. Hammond reached out and held his shoulder.

"It's OK, Alex, it's going to be all right. I'm going back to the village. It's eight twenty-four. With any luck I'll be back with Edward Poole in twenty minutes or so. If he thinks he can get his car up here, I know he'll try it. I'll look in at the cottage on the way down and put Joyce in the picture, and she can phone for an ambulance in case it's worse than we think. Heaven knows how long it's going to take them to get through, though, on roads like this. But at least we'll know they're on their way if we need them. I'll have to take one of the torches."

"Mr. Hammond, are you sure you—"

"Of course. It's the only way. We're wasting time. You

just get that door open. Stay here and wait for me, you two, and give any help you can."

He'd left them. They remained where they were, listening to his footsteps. Then there was silence.

Alex swung back towards the door. They heard him grit his teeth.

"We'll do it. We'll get in there. Once we get behind those hinges the cursed thing'll split wide open. It's a crowbar we need."

"Have you got one?"

"There's one up in the stable-block behind the House. I'll cut round through the paddock."

"D'you want us to come with you?"

"Not both of you. Somebody had better stay put. We can't leave him on his own in this place—if he calls out, I want somebody here." There was a moment's hesitation. Tim and Jamie looked at each other. "Does one of you want to come, or would you rather stick together?"

"We'll stick."

"OK, I won't be five minutes. Keep your ears peeled. If you hear anything, shout to him, tell him help's on the way."

"No problem."

"Thanks." He moved swiftly away down the nave and faded in the darkness beyond.

They remained alone, not speaking. They listened, close by the door, waiting for the cry to come. But no cry came. Only the silence again, and the empty coldness. And high overhead, in the hidden beams, the thin squeak and flutter of night.

They drew nearer together, spoke in whispers.

"How long's he been gone, Jamie?"

"Only three or four minutes. It's just on half past."

"God, it seems like hours. Doc Poole should be here by quarter to or so. I never thought I'd actually be glad to see *him*, but I will tonight."

"Can you hear anything in there?"

"Not a thing. If he does come round, we won't need to listen for him. You could hear a pin drop in this damn place."

"D'you think he's going to be OK?"

"Grandad said he might've had a slight stroke or something. I suppose it mightn't be too serious."

"A stroke? D'you reckon he really believes that?"

"Believing things is his strong point, remember?"

"I wish mine was."

"Me too . . . He's probably right, anyway. Anyone'd have a stroke lugging that . . . that thing up against the door."

"He can't have done that, Tim, not on his own. You saw the size of it, didn't you?"

"How's it supposed to've got there if it wasn't him? There's nobody else in there, is there? And it didn't just get up and walk. Hey, are you OK?"

"Yes . . . sort of."

"What's up?"

"I'd just remembered, that's all . . . I'd forgotten . . . "

"Forgotten what?"

"Why we came here in the first place."

Their eyes met. They turned away together, staring through the twilight. Half hidden in the darkness beyond the archway to the tower, the bell rope dangled down.

In the self-same instant Alex appeared beside it, through the western door, and hurried up the nave to join them.

He had found the crowbar.

"Nothing?"

"Not a sound."

He stripped off his overcoat and fumbled in the pockets.

"We'll need blankets, Tim. Take the ones off my bed, last on the left at the end of the corridor upstairs. And bring a bottle of something strong from the cupboard in the sitting room. Brandy, if you can find it. The lights should still be on to put burglars off the scent but he'll probably have locked up behind him as he always does." He threw Tim a key ring. "Go round by the front drive and use the main door, the ones at the back will be bolted on the inside."

"OK, we'll find everything. Shall we lock up again when we come back?"

"Better not. Leave the front door on the latch. We may have to carry him . . . " He faltered, as if choked with sudden tears.

"Don't worry, Alex. You see to this door, OK? Then it'll all be all right."

Alex couldn't answer. They hurried away. But as they left the church, the crowbar answered for him, biting into wood.

The key fumbled in the lock, not gripping.

"Keep the torch still, Jamie, I can't see what the hell I'm doing."

"I would if I could keep my hand still."

The key ring jangled again. "It's got to be on here somewhere, but it's bound to be the last damn one I try."

"It won't be that one, that's a car key by the look of it."

"Oh come on, you have a go. I can't even feel my fingers. I reckon they've dropped off inside my gloves."

"It's probably this one."

"Oh magic!"

The door swung inward on a wave of yellow warmth. They dived inside it, slamming out the night.

"Heat! I'd forgotten what it felt like. That's the sitting

room on the left, I think. See if you can dig out some brandy somewhere. I'll go and get the blankets."

His footsteps drummed up the staircase at the end of the hallway and off along a corridor somewhere overhead. Jamie remained where he was for an instant, staring around at the hot blind light. Then he forced his feet forward through the sitting-room door.

Another wave of heat welled over him. There was a fire in here, sputtering with logs, but after the hallway the room seemed dim. He knew straight away that he didn't like it. In spite of the warmth here, the place looked cold. Too long for a sitting room; too dead. The cold deadness of hard leather armchairs and furniture heavy with oak. There was only one lamp, on a desk at the farthermost end. The lampshade was dark and two pools of light shone above and below, on ceiling and desktop. The brandy now. He must find the cupboard. He thought he could see what he wanted, beyond the lamp at the end of the room. He made his way over. But before he reached it, he stopped. He had almost trodden on something that must have blown from the desk. He stooped and picked it up. A sheet of paper, half written. He laid it on the desktop and anchored it in place with a bunch of keys. The pool of light spilt across it. He paused and looked down for a moment, frowning.

He didn't hear the footsteps behind him. Tim's voice came, like a blow in the stomach. He started with shock.

"Are you ready, Jamie?"

"What?"

"I said, are you ready? Anything wrong?" The footsteps came nearer. He felt Tim's hand on his shoulder. "What've you found? What's the paper?"

"It must be the book he's doing. It looks like the bit he was writing before he went out."

Tim leaned closer, trying to read.

"I don't see what's so interesting. It's just some stuff about the cottages down in the village. It's not important, is it?"

"No, it's just . . . "

There was a sudden crash behind them. They leapt together and swung round. The room was empty.

Then Tim's body relaxed. He dropped the wad of blankets and moved quickly to the grate.

"God, what a fright. It's one of the logs, that's all. How the hell do we get it back in the fire?"

They managed it together, struggling with the poker and the handle of the hearth-brush, balancing it up into the flames.

"There, that should be OK. We'd better get going. Have you found the brandy?"

"No, I—"

"Hell, Jamie, It's twenty-to already. What've you been doing in here?"

"Oh I don't know. I'm just shattered out of my mind, that's all."

Tim paused, biting his lip. "Sorry, mate. Some vacation it's turned out to be."

"It's not your fault, is it?"

"All the same . . . " Then he grinned. "Thank God you're here, anyway."

"Thanks."

"Look, you grab those blankets. Leave the bottle to me."

They were ready now. They had found what they needed.

"I suppose we ought to switch the lamp off in here. But we'd better leave the hall light on."

The room clicked into gloaming. Only fire-shadows watched them as they rushed away.

5

Even before they reached the western door they could hear the splintered shriek of wood and iron. They found Alex still alone. He was straining at the crowbar, his knee against the door, and was trembling with exertion and with cold.

"OK, Alex? Do you want a hand?"

He didn't pause to answer. He wrenched again. The weight of wood resisted, braced itself against him. But at its edge a slit of light, narrow as a razor, showed them where one hinge had already given way. It couldn't be much longer.

Tim moved to join him.

"We've got the blankets and stuff . . . " He waited, spoke again. "I'll put the brandy down here by the wall, OK? What about the keys? Shall I put them in your coat?"

The wrenching ceased. Alex turned towards him, one shoulder slumped against the door frame. His face was haggard, stiff with rust and sweat.

"What? What did you say?"

"The keys, Alex."

For an instant the eyes were blank. He raised his arm and wiped his sleeve across them. Then, slowly, understanding seemed to dawn. "Oh yes, thanks, I'd better have them." He slipped them in his pocket and looked around him. "Well done for finding the things, both of you. And you left the door on the latch?"

"No problem."

"Full marks." He drew a breath, then swung away. "Right, this damn thing had better start saying its prayers. Its number's up."

He lunged and struck, heaving the crowbar back across his chest, then struck and heaved again. Wood ruptured. From top to bottom the hinge-side of the door was gashed with brightness. The screws had lost their hold.

"That's got it! Shoulders should do the rest."

He threw the crowbar from him and the flagstones rang with echoes. Outside, as if in answer, another sound rang back. A car horn. The stutter of an engine, and the swish of tires on ice. Then headlamps strafed the darkness, and skeletons of windows went scuttling down the nave. Voices now, and footsteps, round beyond the chapel, and a sudden eye of torchlight at the western door. Mr. Hammond had returned.

He hurried through the church towards them.

"Sorry, Alex, it took longer than I thought. It's worse than ever underfoot."

"Where's the doctor? You've brought him, haven't you?"

"Don't worry, I showed him the window on our way round. He'll be here in a couple of seconds."

"Is Uncle still . . . ?"

"Yes, still in the same position. No sound from him, I suppose?"

"No. Nothing."

"Never mind, we'll soon have him out of there. You've done a great job on this by the look of it." He stripped off his overcoat and moved to the crypt, pressing firmly on the wood with his palms. It winced at his touch. "One good thrust from the three of us together could shift it now if we're lucky, as long as the stone's not wedged. If it's only resting, it should topple."

Suddenly Alex froze. His face was white against the shadows.

"God, I've just thought. What if . . . The stone might . . . "

"No, there's not a chance of that. If we put force enough behind it we'll knock it a mile clear . . . Come on, let's get it over with—here's Edward now."

Jamie didn't turn. He couldn't. But he heard the doctor's footsteps in the emptiness behind him. They drew level, passed him. A black-gloved hand dropped something even blacker on the flagstones; it thudded limply with a clink of tiny bottles. A quick exchange of voices, tense and urgent. The figures moving backward from the doorway. Pausing. Tautening together . . .

They sprang. With a blow that shook the church to its foundations their bodies jolted back. For an instant the door hung gaping, crooked as a tooth, then it ripped from its socket, leaping inward, with a squeal of wood on stone.

It was only a second before the crash came, less time than it takes for a camera shutter to blink. But in that single second, Jamie saw.

He saw the door and the stone suspended together, unmoving in dazzling space. And the steps and the floor of the crypt far below them, poised to receive their weight. He saw the other things too, just as he'd seen them before from the window: the camp-light and pickaxe, the black iron shovel, the body stretched out by the oblong of earth. The same sprawling huddle of dark brown greatcoat and the same bunch of keys by the outstretched arm. But the floor had turned round now, fixed in a new line of vision, and showed him one thing it had hidden before. It showed him the head. It was tipped, lying sideways, facing the doorway.

Then the camera shutter crashed down.

Its impact was monstrous. A headlong impact of stone against stone, thundering out volley after volley of echoes up through the chapel, the nave, and the tower. And then there was nothing but stillness again, and the choking gray blindess of dust.

Dr. Poole was the first to move forward. With his handkerchief pressed to his mouth he groped his way into the crypt. Mr. Hammond made to follow then hung back on the second step down, his hand gripped tight on Alex's shoulder, forcing him to a standstill. They waited.

In the doorway Jamie waited too, with Tim beside him.

The dust settled in a thin shroud. The camp-light emerged again, watching. Crouched at the end of his shadow, Dr. Poole examined the body. Then, slowly, he got to his feet.

Alex broke free of the hand that held him and rushed down the steps with the vicar on his heels. Dr. Poole turned to face him, but his eyes were lowered.

"I'm sorry, Alex."

For a moment Alex stared at him, then thrust him aside with a stifled cry. He threw himself down by the body, clutching it to him as if begging it to speak, to move. But only the dust moved in answer.

Jamie watched, too cold now for feeling. He watched Mr. Hammond kneel down too and slip his arm round Alex. Then ease him up, and help him forward to the steps.

"Come on, Alex. Up into the nave. There's nothing you can do here. I saw some brandy up there, didn't I? It's what we both need."

They came up towards him, brushed against him. But he didn't move. He smelt the breath of the crypt as they passed him, like the breath of old cellars. The doctor was standing stockstill now, his eyes strangely fixed on the body at his feet. He didn't look up until Mr. Hammond had returned to his side. They spoke in low voices.

"I think Alex'll be all right, I've put one of the blankets round him. We'll get him back to the House in a minute."

"I've got something in my bag that'll help him sleep. Perhaps we could fetch Mrs. Gregson up here, she could stay the night with him."

"I shouldn't think she'll need fetching. The whole village must have heard the din by now."

"What on earth was the old chap *doing* in here, David?"

The vicar shook his head. He looked drained and bewildered.

"I don't know. I only know what I told you in the car. The whole business seems crazy beyond belief. It *can't* have anything to do with what he wanted to tell me tonight, that'd only make it crazier still. And yet why else should he have come here? And if that *is* what he was intending all along, why didn't he give anyone any hint of it? When Mrs. Gregson left him on his own there at quarter to six, she said he was still writing happily at his desk. He can't have given her any indication of what he was planning or she'd have told us."

"Do you think he *was* planning it by then?"

"What else can I think? He had to have the keys from the dining room to get in here and he certainly didn't take them between six and seven, did he, with a full Committee meeting going on?" He stooped and picked them up from beside the body, jangling them helplessly in his palm. "So when in heaven's name *did* he take them?"

"Are you sure they're the ones from the cottage?"

"Well, of course I'm sure. There *is* only one set, and I'm not likely to mistake keys of this age. I recognized them the minute I looked through the window. They haven't been out of our possession since we came to Lychwood."

Dr. Poole glanced round, frowning.

"Did he bring all this other stuff with him too?"

"He must have. I presume everything's come from the House. I haven't seen the lamp and pickaxe before, but the shovel's certainly his, it's one of a pair from his sitting-room grate. Though God alone knows what he was planning to do with it."

"I'd have thought that's pretty obvious."

"But *why?* And how could he have shifted that . . . that appalling thing on his own? He was an old man."

"I'm afraid that's something he won't be able to tell us now."

They gazed down together at the silent figure.

"It's senseless, Edward. Uncanny. As if he came here on his own to play some kind of grotesque game with that legend. Even the bell was . . . " He faltered, shook his head. "Can you tell how long he's been dead?"

"I'm no expert on this sort of thing, believe me. But it's certainly not more than an hour."

Jamie moved for the first time. The words drew his eyes to his wrist. Even before he read what it showed him, he knew. It was almost nine o'clock.

Mr. Hammond's voice came again.

"I suppose it was a heart attack?"

"I . . . I'm not sure, David."

"Not sure? It can't have been anything else, can it?"

"That won't be for me to decide. But you've noticed the back of his head, haven't you? The contusion?"

"Contusion?"

"When he fell perhaps. But it must have been the most devilish knock to cause bruising like that."

They turned together, obscuring the body with their stooping backs. There was silence now in the chapel and for the first time other sounds became clear, sounds coming closer, up from the village. Footsteps on the pathway, and frost-sharp voices.

The two men heard them too. Abruptly, the doctor straightened. His tone was changed, almost urgent.

"David, listen to me. Tell me quickly, before they get here. Can you swear he was alone in here?"

"Alone? You know he was. You looked through the window yourself."

"I thought I might have been wrong, that's all."

"Well, of course you weren't wrong. Who else is supposed to have been here? And where, for goodness sake? There isn't exactly anywhere to hide, is there? What on earth makes you—"

"What about the window?"

"The window? It wasn't even open. I told you, we had to smash the thing out of the wall. And look at it! It's fifteen feet from the floor! And not even wide enough to get more than your head through. Who could get through a thing that size? But why are you—"

"David, the door—it *was* locked, wasn't it?"

"Locked? What in heaven's name—"

"Tell me, *was* it?"

"Good God, man, see for yourself—do you think an unlocked door would rip open a door frame like that? Look, what *is* all this?"

The footsteps had grown sharper, were almost at the

tower. Calls came. Questions. The doctor relaxed now. He looked strangely relieved.

"I'm sorry, it's nothing. I simply needed to hear you say it. To put my mind at rest or something like that."

"Edward, I don't understand."

"It was seeing that fearful contusion on the back of his head, probably. There seems no doubt now that he must have done it when he fell, but a moment ago it just looked horribly wrong."

"Wrong? Why?"

"I suppose because it *is* on the back of his head. But if it does turn out to be the cause of death, he must have moved since he did it, that's all. It's not impossible."

"Moved?"

"Well, look at him, David. He's lying chest downward . . . "

For a second the words seemed to jolt up at Jamie and topple him sideways. He clutched at Tim for support. Figures moved across his vision, pushed past him, figures he was dimly aware that he knew. Mrs. Gregson. Old Wilkie. Joe. But he didn't see them. He was looking beyond them, down at the floor of the crypt. Dr. Poole and the vicar had stepped out of focus, away from the gas lamp, and its blinding white glare had returned. And, within it, just three spots of darkness began to take shape. Still lying apart from each other, yet linked now, connected together, as if the words of the doctor had locked them in place. He stared at them, seeing the pattern they showed him. The oblong of earth. The black shovel. The head.

They blurred into one and grew suddenly larger. The chapel spun round and there was nothing but night.

6

---◆---

Neither Tim nor Jamie went home on the following day. They slept, for fourteen hours, until noon. Beyond the window of their bedroom, unseen and unheard, the machinery of the law began to move.

A car brought a detective inspector, a police surgeon and photographer just after ten. At eleven a pathologist drove up past the cottage to join them. A mortuary van followed at midnight. The body was taken away.

In the morning a coroner opened an inquest. Alex was there, to establish identification; the pathologist confirmed that a blow to the head had caused death.

At tea, the detective inspector came back to the cottage to question the two boys alone. They answered his questions as well as they could, describing the events they recalled. But they recalled very little. The events were too close to be looked at clearly, too real to be looked at at all.

Later, he came down to London, asked the same questions, and returned there in April to ask them again. They gave the same answers, brief and unhelpful. The things that had happened were too far away now; they'd begun to seem almost unreal.

They waited for summer.

Letters came from the vicar, addressed to Tim's father, but Tim was told little of what they contained. This year, for the first summer ever, there was no invitation to Lychwood: the place was unsettled, the police were still there.

They waited again.

The autumn term ended. No invitation arrived from the cottage; the prospect of New Year in Norfolk looked dim. And then, in December, it finally happened: both Jamie and Tim would be welcome to come. The police had departed. A second full inquest had just been concluded; the case was now over, officially closed.

There had been no solution. The crypt had refused to surrender its secret; Mr. Jefford now lay beneath six feet of earth. Just three facts were proved beyond possible question: no human creature could enter the chapel except through the doorway; the door had been locked with the keys by the body; the death-blow was struck by the shovel alone.

No clues were forthcoming. The verdict was final. *Murder by person or persons unknown.*

PART II

7

---◆---

Tim's voice came backwards through the window in a rush of late December air.

"Can you see him, Jamie? He said he'd be here with the car."

"Give the train a chance, we haven't even reached the platform yet."

"I bet he'll be really knocked out seeing us in a first-class compartment."

"So will we, probably, if the ticket inspector shows up."

"He's not likely to now. I expect Sunday's his day off. Anyway, where's your sense of adventure gone?"

"I'm saving it up for when we get there. I reckon I'm going to need it."

Tim's head squeezed back into the carriage, away from the tousling wind. "Hey, don't forget—not a word about you-know-what, OK? Not till we've scoped out how the land lies."

"Course not. I'm not that thick."

"OK, OK, just checking. As long as we play it cool to start off with, Grandad'll probably give us all the info we need." His eyes sparkled with sudden excitement. "You wait, this is going to be the vacation of all time."

"I haven't got over the last one yet."

"You'd better get a move on then, the next one's just starting—here's the platform coming up. We're almost there."

Jamie leapt up beside him and thrust his head clear of the glass, out into the coldness beyond. They were almost there. A few minutes from now Mr. Hammond would be with them. The car would take them deep into the emptiness of Norfolk. And when they stopped, Lychwood would be waiting—

"There he is! Over in the car park! *Grandad!*" Tim whooped a frantic greeting from the window. Beyond the railing Mr. Hammond raised his arm in recognition. "Stick where you are, Grandad! We'll be right with you!" He swung away, snatching up the parkas and sweaters, and rushed towards the door. "Move it, Jamie. The train only stops here about ten seconds. Bring the rucksacks and wellies, OK?"

"What?"

"The rest of the luggage, dodo."

"Hell, Tim—"

"Come on!"

He vanished. Jamie followed with the baggage, bundling his way along the corridor outside. By the time he turned the corner, Tim had disappeared again.

Farther down the train, doors were drumming out a warning of departure. He leapt down on the platform and dragged the bags and boots behind him, cursing Tim to blazes underneath his breath. Footsteps came towards him.

"Come on, lad. She's going."

He looked up blankly. "What?"

"She's going. You'll miss her if you don't step on it."

"Oh . . . Oh no, it's OK thanks. I've just got off."

"Oh, I see." The guard chuckled. "As long as you're sure. This is your last chance to change your mind." He slammed the door and raised his hand towards his mouth.

Crouched among the litter of the luggage, Jamie watched and listened. A whistle split the air. The train responded with a sudden backwards jolting, as if reluctant to be gone without him, a final indication that he still could change his mind. Then, slowly, it slipped forward. It gathered speed and left him.

Another whistle sounded from the car park. He turned his head towards it. With his arm around Tim's shoulders Mr. Hammond waved a welcome, beckoned him to join them, and yelled how glad he was to see them back again. Jamie waved in answer. He hoisted up the luggage and raced towards the gate.

Even before he could be certain how he'd got there, he was wedged between the rucksacks in the rear seat of the car. They turned northward from the little country station. The final houses ran alongside for a moment, then decided not to follow and fell away behind. They were on their own now, in an endlessness of space.

Jamie watched it from the window. A rolling swell of whiteness, threaded through with hedgerows, broken at the skyline by the skeletons of pines. This was Norfolk, exactly as he'd seen it first, a year ago today. He spread his arms wide open on the rucksacks and let it rush to meet him.

"Thanks for the invite, Mr. Hammond. It's great to be back."

"It's great to have you, Jamie."

"I can't wait to see the cottage again."

"It hasn't changed."

"Nothing ever does up here, does it?"

"No, always just the same. It's too old to change. Like me. I'm really glad you like it."

"It's magic."

The old, familiar magic. He wondered if he'd ever know what its magic really was. He watched again, trying to decipher the secret of its spell. Its emptiness perhaps; empty earth and empty sky. It looked so open, after London. But it wasn't, not really. It was deeper than London. A hidden landscape, silent and withdrawn.

The car swept on across it, seaward.

Behind the brightness of their conversation a darker shadow hovered, waiting to be summoned. But none of them would name it. They spoke of safer things.

"Did you and Gran have a good Christmas?"

"Busy, as usual. I did a Midnight Service this year, as well as all the regular ones."

"Terrific. Any jackpot collections?"

"Tim, you really are turning into a nasty little materialist, aren't you?"

"'Fraid so. Sick, isn't it? Still, that's the modern world for you. Actually, I'm thinking of opting out soon and joining Greenpeace or something. Hey, by the way, thanks for the Christmas cash, it was dead generous."

"Not too sick for you, was it?"

"Oh no, that's OK. I'm not reckoning on opting out quite yet. Probably just before exams."

"What did you get with it? Something your mum and dad didn't approve of, I hope."

"You bet. A Sony Walkman."

"Never heard of it."

"Come off it, Grandad, you're not that much of a wrinkly yet."

"You tell your gran that."

"How is she?"

"Oh, bearing up pretty well. She was up to her eyes in scones and jam when I left. She's convinced you never get anything but junk food in London."

"Good old Gran. And . . . and how's the rest of Lychwood doing? Alex and Gregson and everybody?"

The shadow shifted slightly, moved forward to the light. Mr. Hammond sensed it from the corner of his eye, but didn't turn to meet it.

"Oh, you'll see for yourself soon enough. Well, Jamie, what about you? Did you and your mum have a good Christmas?"

The moment passed. Other shadows came, less dark but more real, seeping slowly upward from the fields, downward from the sky. The vicar clicked a switch; the road turned yellow in the headlamps. The shadows moved in closer. Jamie watched them come.

"It gets dark earlier up here, Mr. Hammond. Than in London, I mean."

"Not really. You just notice it more."

"It'll be night by tea-time."

"Twilight, anyway."

"Yes."

Yes, twilight. That was it. Norfolk was twilight. Not really seen at all, only guessed at. Half-glimpses sometimes, when you weren't quite looking; slipping into hiding when you looked too hard. A landscape that watched you from behind your shoulder; when you turned around to catch it, it was behind your back again.

"Eyes left at the top of the slope, you two. First sight of home."

They craned forward. The car thrummed up towards the

ridge and cleared it, swinging to the right. To their left the land swept downward through graying fields and pasture, to meet the sky far out. And where they met there lay a band of deeper grayness like a narrow overlapping, half hidden by the dunes.

"The sea! And there's Lychwood!"

Jamie saw it, a nest of lights below them, ringed about with trees. He saw the other line of trees too, reaching out beyond the last lights of the village, tiny now, and darker than the rest. He followed them, saw them winding westward through an open stretch of grassland, and knew where they would lead him. An avenue of beeches. He had followed them before. He left the path unfinished and turned his head. He glanced at Tim. Tim had seen them too, though he didn't have to say so. His stillness said it for him, without the need of words.

A hush fell on them all now. The twilight thickened as the car dropped down towards the village. Trees came, and the first outlying farmsteads. Then the sign announcing Lychwood; the corner-shop and baker's; Mr. Hammond's church, St. Andrew's, across the village green. The high street climbed again, the house straggled out and dwindled. There were lights in every window that they passed. Dr. Poole's on the right, with its office extension. The Wilkies' little cottage of weatherbeaten flint. Mrs. Gregson's on the left, set back beyond its garden, darkly overshadowed by a copse of ancient pines . . . Jamie stared. They were all still here, then. Just as they had been throughout the year that he had spent in London. It seemed so strange. In London, they hadn't been quite real. That was why the plans he'd made with Tim had seemed so easy, like a game—

"Hold tight! Here we go!"

His body was flung sideways as the tires bit on gravel.

They had left the road behind them and had turned into the lane. Lights beckoned. The car swept on to meet them and drew level, then clicked off into silence at the gate.

"Gran!"

A square of orange warmth had fallen out across the garden. Mrs. Hammond stood in silhouette, tall against the light. Tim struggled from his seat belt and leapt out. Jamie watched him for an instant as he ran towards the doorway, and felt suddenly half happy, half afraid. He turned his eyes aside from the little patch of brightness and stared into the dark that lay beyond. Somewhere out there, a secret still lay buried, the secret that the two of them were planning to unearth. . . . Tim had reached his gran and was wrapped inside her arms now. He looked oddly, almost comically, young. Too young, for what they were intending. This wasn't just a game now. It was real.

"Shift yourself, Jamie! You're here!"

He hoisted himself forward from his seat between the rucksacks, pushed the car door open and slipped out. His feet touched earth. The year had come full circle and brought him back to Lychwood. Too late to change his mind now. He was here.

"I can't believe this is really true, Jamie."

"You can say that again."

"It seems *years* since I last saw this place. It's because of missing out the summer probably. Here's the green coming up—we've got time for a quick walk round it before we head back but we'd better not be later than nine. Gran reckons we both need an early night after the journey and everything."

"She's not far wrong. I'm shattered."

"Me too. It's the sea air."

"Sea air? We've only been out about fifteen minutes."

"It's pretty lethal stuff. Hey, let's go and try and see what's in Carter's window—I fancy getting one of those sailing-smock things if they've got them."

"They're a bit yuppie, aren't they? You'll be in green wellies next."

They made their way across the darkened green and peered in at the windows of the shops, their faces pressed against the glass.

"It's exactly the same stuff they had last year. I don't reckon they ever sell anything up here." Jamie fell back and stood for a moment gazing round at the quietness of it all. The whole place seemed deserted. "It's really weird to think we were in a coffee bar in London this time yesterday, isn't it?"

Tim turned too, and looked at him. Beneath its brashness, his voice was edged with apprehension. "Hey, you're not sorry you came, are you?"

"No, *course* I'm not. It's really great seeing your gran and grandad again. You're dead lucky having them."

"I know." The note of apprehension sharpened. "D'you reckon they've changed at all, Jamie?"

"How d'you mean?"

"Well, to look at."

Jamie hesitated. So Tim had seen it too. It wasn't really surprising. The change was evident enough.

"Perhaps they have, a bit. They look . . . well, I don't know really. Sort of older."

Tim slumped down against the window, half squatting on the narrow wooden sill. When he spoke, all his brashness had gone from him. His sudden misery was startling. "They look bloody ancient."

"Oh come on, Tim, that's—"

"You know they do, so why not say so? They've aged about twenty years in twelve months. And you know why, too. It's this business with Old Jefford. They haven't said anything, they're pretending it's all OK now. But it isn't. It's really rotting them up." He faltered. Then his voice took on a note that Jamie hadn't ever heard in it before. Deep earnestness perhaps. Or fear. "I've got to do something, Jamie. I'm going to have a go, anyway. I wasn't sure, on the way here in the car. It seems so different somehow. From when we talked about it all in London, I mean."

"I know."

"But I am sure now. I'm going to do it. I'm going ahead with what we planned. Will you help me?"

Jamie drew a long breath. "Yes," he said.

There was a moment's stillness. Tim broke it with his familiar grin.

"Thanks."

It was over. They left the window and headed back across the green, turning up their collars against the cold winter air. They climbed the road together, passing by the houses of the people that they'd talked about in London. But not talking now. Talking would come later. Tomorrow.

They stopped only once, just before they left the roadway, at the corner of the lane to the cottage and the Grounds. Neither of them needed to speak what he was thinking, each of them knew that the thought he had was shared: whoever, whatever, had dealt out death in Lychwood, was still here, somewhere near them, even now . . . Jamie started, raised his hand towards his cheek. Something soft had touched it, as cold as a moth. He looked up.

"It's snowing."

"I thought it was. Fantastic. Thank heavens we came today."

"Why?"

"We could be cut off by tomorrow, that's why."

"Cut off? Are you serious?"

"Course I am. It often happens up here, if the snow *really* comes. I missed the beginning of the term twice."

"D'you mean we won't be able to get out?"

"We'll be able to get out of the cottage OK, if we do a bit of spadework. Not out of the village, though." He grinned suddenly. "I hope it *does* come. It'll make things easier, won't it? Sort of narrow the circle. You know—no escape."

"Yes, I suppose it will. With us inside it."

" 'Fraid so."

And they ran, back to the shelter of the cottage, through the flakes of falling night.

8

━━━━━ ◆ ━━━━━

Jamie was woken by light. Midday light, he thought, dazzlingly clear. He listened, waiting for some sound of life from the kitchen down below. But no sound came. No movement touched the cottage. He sat up startled, blinking at his watch. It was only eight o'clock.

He glanced across the room. Tim was still in bed, a tousled hump of blankets. With a mixture of relief and wonder, he reached towards the window and pulled the curtain back. He stared. The world had been turned over. The sky was mud-thick, clogged with grayness, the light came from the earth.

The snow had come. Everything lay buried. The Grounds had wrapped themselves inside it, as if inside a shroud. Featureless now, hummocked and silent. Only the trees protruded, and the white-hooded tower.

The hump of blankets stirred and grunted. Tim's face appeared above it, blurred with hair and sleep. He knuckled at his eyes.

"What time is it?"

"Eight."

"*Eight?*" He fell back with a groan. "Hell, Jamie, that's

the middle of the night. What're you *doing*, for pity's sake? Why can't you just sleep, like normal people?"

"Come and look at this."

"At what?"

There was a pause. Then something in the tone of Jamie's voice seemed to spark the blankets into movement. They left the bed and lumbered to the window, with Tim still tight inside them.

"I don't *believe* it, Jamie!" He whistled. "Will you look at *that*!"

"I am. D'you reckon we're cut off?"

"Oh, I shouldn't think so, not yet. The main road's probably still OK—but it's not bad, is it, for a start?"

"A start? You must be joking. I've never seen so much of the stuff."

"You wait. If we get another load on top of this lot, it'll be *really* worth seeing. And we're going to, I reckon. Just look at that sky!"

Jamie looked. Tim was right. More snow was on its way. The sky was sagging with it, like a paunch. It would touch the land soon, burst its contents out across it.

They turned. Another voice had joined them.

"Hello, you two. I thought I heard you up and about. I've brought you a cup of tea."

"Great."

Still in dressing gown and slippers, Mrs. Hammond moved across the room and set a tray down on the sill. "So, another Norfolk miracle."

"It's fantastic, isn't it? It must've chucked it down all night."

"I didn't mean the snow. I meant you being up at eight o'clock."

"Part of my new macho image, Gran."

"You can both get the spades out later and have a go at the lane."

"We'll never shift this lot!"

"Good heavens, the new image was a bit short-lived, wasn't it? Anyhow, you know Monday afternoon's Joe's day for bringing up the groceries from the village, and he can't be expected to drive through a foot of snow. So it's spade-work and supper, or no spadework and no supper. It's up to you."

"Enough said. Are you . . . are you reckoning on going out yourself this morning, Gran?"

Jamie looked across at him, struck by the sudden hesitation in his voice. Then he remembered. Monday morning. There was the same hesitation in Mrs. Hammond too, before she replied.

"No . . . no, of course not. Where on earth am I supposed to be going in weather like this? Now look lively and get some clothes on, unless you intend to wear blankets for breakfast."

She left them. Her footsteps hurried away down the stairs. They looked at the place where she'd been, then at each other. Jamie put their thought into words.

"She's not going up there, then, for her Monday clean-round."

"Doesn't look like it."

"It might be just the snow. I mean, it's not exactly the weather for mucking out old churches, is it? Or . . . or maybe she doesn't fancy it, after what happened."

"Maybe."

"She didn't seem too keen to discuss it, did she?"

Tim didn't answer for a moment. He bit his nail in silence. When he finally glanced up, some of yesterday's tension had come back into his voice. "She's *got* to discuss it, Jamie. Or one of them has. We can't go on avoiding it all like this, we've only got a week. We've just got to get hold of some facts to get started on, or we're really sunk."

But, in the event, he needn't have worried. Before the afternoon was out they were to have learnt all they wanted to know, and more.

They worked hard on the lane all morning, shifting its burden aside into two high banks at the edges. When they finally reached it, the road was still clear, a wet black ribbon on whiteness. But the first flakes were falling even before they were home.

After lunch the clockwork routine of the cottage clicked back into motion. Mrs. Hammond had shut herself off in the kitchen, surrounded by washing; the vicar was out on his regular round of the parish. Last year the boys had gone with him; but this year their legs were too tired to move. They played Scrabble on the dining-room table.

"You can't put *that* down, Tim! What if your gran comes in?"

"It's the only word I've got."

"You mean it's the only word you know."

"She won't come in anyway, she never leaves the kitchen when she's washing. And even if she did, she probably wouldn't know what it meant. Vicars' wives aren't like that."

"I didn't think vicars' grandsons were till I met you."

"It gives me thirteen anyway. Which means I'm still going to lose. Just great." He flopped back with a groan. "I don't reckon I'll be able to move my shoulders for *years*. One thing's for sure—if the snow strikes again, it can stay there."

"What about your gran's catch-22? No spadework, no supper."

"Don't worry. Joe delivers enough for the week." He turned his head suddenly, wincing at the pain of it. "This is him now by the sound of it. It looks as if our slog's done *some* good anyhow."

The swish of the van came closer and stopped. The cottage door opened on a flurry of snowflakes. Beyond the dining room Joe Wilkie appeared in the hallway, a cardboard box clutched to his chest. Tim called to him as he passed on his way to the kitchen.

"Hi, Joe. D'you want a hand?"

Joe paused for a moment, startled by a voice he hadn't expected to hear there. Then he grinned. He spoke slowly, like someone who didn't get on too well with words.

"Oh hello, Tim. Jamie. I'd forgotten. No, that's OK. There's only the three."

"Great. I don't reckon I could even lift a matchbox after all that spadework up the lane."

"You did a good job, then. I was wondering, before I got here. With the van and all."

He moved on, speaking with Mrs. Hammond for a minute in the kitchen. Then two more trips through the hallway, and he grinned again and was gone.

Jamie listened to the slow dying of tires. "Not much of a talker, is he?"

"Oh, Joe's all right. He's brighter than he makes out. He's a bit of a one for the nightlife too."

"What? Joe?"

"So Grandad says."

"I wouldn't have thought there's much nightlife round Lychwood."

"There's a bit in Norwich though."

"What sort does he go for?"

"Gambling dens and stuff like that. Shows he's got his head screwed on the right way, anyhow. I wish he'd take me with him."

"They'd want to see the color of your cash first. You weren't exactly very flush on Saturday night, were you, when I had to fork out for the coffees?"

"So what? Nor's Joe, from what Grandad said, but it doesn't stop him. And speak of the devil . . ."

"Thanks, Tim. Just the sort of greeting a vicar appreciates." The front door had opened again. Mr. Hammond had appeared in the hallway, shaking off a thick fleece of snow from his topcoat and hat. "Well, we're in for another night of it by all accounts. The high street's already looking pretty grim. It's lucky for Alex he isn't back at the office till next week—he'll never get the car down from the High House, and he couldn't rely on the buses to Wells in this weather."

Mrs. Hammond's voice came from the kitchen. "Is that you, David? Say when you're ready for tea, the three of you. The kettle's on."

"Thanks, Joyce, we're ready now, once I've washed my hands."

"Shall we go through to the kitchen, Grandad? Gran'll probably want to keep an eye on the washing at the same time."

"No . . . No, I'll bring it through here. You needn't move the Scrabble as long as there's room for the three of us."

"Isn't Gran . . . ?"

"No. Don't worry, we've discussed it already. She's in the picture." He moved away upstairs.

Tim frowned. "What was all that about? What picture? Are we in for a ticking-off or what?"

"Beats me. We probably *will* be, though, if you don't put that Scrabble away."

"Oh, God!" Tim swept the contents of the board back into the box and watched his last word collapse into innocent parts. Then he stirred them again to make sure.

They waited.

When Mr. Hammond brought the tea, he closed the door to the hallway behind him before he sat down. He looked at them for a moment in silence, as if wondering where to begin.

"Well, let's get this over with as fast as we can, shall we?"

"Get what over, Grandad? Is it something we've done?"

"Yes, I suppose it is in a way." He smiled. "Or rather, something you haven't done, which your gran and I want to say thanks for."

"Thanks? For what?"

"For not mentioning last year."

Tim caught his breath. "Oh. Oh, I see."

"Especially when we could see how much you were both bursting with it. And it's only natural that you should have been."

Tim recovered slightly. "Why didn't *you* mention it then, Grandad? You or Gran?"

"To be honest, Tim, we didn't want the whole terrible business dragged up at random every minute of the day. So we arranged we'd wait for a good quiet few minutes when I could get you on your own together and have the matter out once and for all. It's only fair that I should." He paused, watching them, waiting for their comment. Neither of them spoke. "So I propose to give you the facts as I know them, and you can ask any questions you like. If I can answer them, I promise I will. But there's one thing I'd like to ask you both in return. I'm sure you'll understand."

"Of course. Anything."

"I'd just like to feel that—once we leave this room—the whole affair's closed between us for good. I don't want it to spoil this week, especially for your gran. We've had enough of it, both of us."

"Has it . . . has it been bad, Grandad?"

Mr. Hammond's eyes turned aside. He passed his hand across them. When he answered, his voice was quiet.

"Yes. It's been hell, Tim. There's no other word for it."

They didn't need to ask any more. They could see the hell that he'd been through, in the gray shadows on his face.

He shook his head and looked up, smiling again. "But that sort of talk's not going to help. Let's get on with what we're here for. I'll make it as short as I can, and you interrupt when you like. And then we forget it, OK?"

"OK."

"Right. The question is, where do we start?"

"The beginning's not a bad place."

"It wouldn't be, if I knew where the beginning was. How much do you know already?"

"Not much at all really. Not about after we left."

"OK, let's start there." He fell silent. They watched him and knew what it was costing him, to look back. Then he seemed to make up his mind. "After the first inquest the police really moved in. That was when it became pretty obvious to all of us that they weren't satisfied it was just some terrible accident, and nothing I could say seemed to make any difference. After the pathologist's report, you see, there was no doubt that old Mr. Jefford's head had been . . . had been in contact with the shovel. And that contact was apparently why he died. Well, you saw the chapel yourselves. There was no way in which it *could* have been anything but an accident, but . . . but the police kept coming back, again and again. They took away the keys and sealed the place up, and questioned us all for months on end. They even went down to London, I hear?"

"Yes, twice. But we weren't much help, really. It seemed hard to sort of remember things down there. What did they ask you and Gran?"

"Oh, nearly always about the keys. Yet the facts were straightforward enough. Your gran locked up after her clean-round on the Monday morning, and the place when she left it was just as it'd always been. She'd even unlocked the crypt and had a look in. When she came back here, she hung the keys inside the cupboard over there, where they're always put for safe keeping, and didn't leave the cottage again once. Yet at eight o'clock when the . . . when I looked for them, they'd gone."

"Who knew they were there—apart from us, I mean?"

"Only the Church Committee members. I can swear to that. Not a soul but them . . . Oh, and old Mr. Jefford himself, of course. Somehow or other he must have come in and got them, for whatever crazy idea he had in mind. But *when*, I don't know. Our front door wasn't locked, but even so . . . Anyway, the fact remains that those were the keys that were used to open the place up, both the west door and the crypt. The police are quite certain of that much."

"What else did they discover?"

"A few things that seem obvious enough. The pickaxe we saw had definitely been used to lever up the stone, and they found traces on the floor to show where the stone itself had been 'walked' across it, upright—rocked from corner to corner to shift it up to the steps. Mr. Jefford must have done it, I suppose, though heaven alone knows how an old man . . ." He shrugged. "That was one of the things that puzzled the police too, I think. How he'd done it, I mean. Apart from the few obvious bits and pieces he had in his pockets—handkerchief and penknife and house- and car-keys and the like—he hadn't brought anything with him except the stuff we saw on the floor. So the police drew a blank. He'd managed it somehow, yet the whole business seemed impossible."

In spite of himself, Jamie shivered. "Were there any foot-prints, Mr. Hammond? Near the . . . near the middle of the floor?"

"None that you wouldn't expect. Before we broke in, I suppose there were only mine, as I was the only one who ever went right down there—and not very often at that. And old Mr. Jefford's own. But the dust we made would have covered all those. After that, half the village arrived and traipsed round there."

"And fingerprints, Grandad? On . . . on the shovel, I mean?"

"Why do you ask that?"

"I . . . I'm not sure. Well, because of the verdict, I sup-pose."

"The verdict, yes . . . Anyway, the answer's easy enough: just the prints you'd expect, considering it was kept in the grate at the High House, and even those were pretty smudged. Just old Mr. Jefford's and Mrs. Gregson's, I think, from what the police said."

"How did you get all this info out of them?"

Mr. Hammond smiled for the first time since he'd begun. "Vicars have a knack of being told things. And the detective inspector was friendly enough. He owed me a few expla-nations, anyway, for plaguing me like he did for no apparent reason. It looked enough like an accident to me, and I told him so."

"What *did* you tell him exactly?"

"That the old fellow had had a bad fall, of course, and knocked the back of his head on the shovel. Edward Poole said as much at the time."

"So why didn't the police think so too? Why did they think it was . . ."

Tim shied at the word. As if forcing himself, Mr. Hammond drew a breath and named it for him. "Murder." It fell darkly across the brightness of the room. The shadow had emerged now, come out into the light. "I don't know, Tim. I suppose because the whole situation looked so uncanny, for an accident. What they wouldn't accept was that any other possibility was even more crazy, given the facts. How could there possibly have been a motive, for one thing? The poor old chap mightn't have been very popular with anybody but that's hardly a reason, is it? As far as I can see, nobody stood to gain at all, apart from financially, and if *that's* what they thought . . ." His lips tightened. He looked nearer to anger than Jamie had ever seen him. "The truth of the matter is that they were at their wits' end, desperate for *any* easy solution to wrap the case up. If they could've pinned it on Alex as next of kin or on Mrs. Gregson even, for the ten thousand quid the poor woman was left in the will, they'd probably have done it and gladly, to save their own faces. And to hell with anybody's feelings."

He halted for an instant, as if shocked by the force of his words. His anger subsided slightly. But they could still hear it, just beneath the surface. "Anyway, it became clear by the autumn that they'd found out all they were going to and that they were starting to scale down their inquiries. They must have made their report to the coroner at the beginning of this month, and he called a second inquest almost at once. You know the final verdict, based I suppose on the pathologist's post-mortem and a forensic examination of . . . of traces found on the back of the shovel. A scandalous verdict, in my opinion, with no real proof at all. Well, be that as it may. We had a funeral service in St. Andrew's a fortnight ago, but I made sure it was as quiet as possible: only Alex as 'family' and a handful of people from the village. And, above all, no confounded reporters hanging around. And that, as far as the police are concerned, is that. They've given us their verdict and gone back where they came from, leaving us to pick up the pieces as best we can."

His anger left him. Weariness came in its place, sudden and gray beneath his eyes. He closed them, and sank back in his chair. "I'm sorry, both of you, I think I'd rather we called it a day now if that's OK. There's no more I can tell you anyway."

They watched him, saw the effort he'd been making. Tim spoke, with an attempt at brightness.

"Fine. Thanks for . . . for talking to us. You're OK, Grandad, aren't you?"

Mr. Hammond nodded, his eyes still closed. They got awkwardly to their feet. Jamie moved across to the door and glanced back. Tim hadn't followed. He'd paused on his way past his grandfather's chair and was behind him now, looking down.

"I'm dead sorry, Grandad, about what you've been through and everything. I really am."

The vicar nodded again. Still he didn't open his eyes. He looked drained and wretched.

"Yes. The whole business has got me down. It's got the whole village down. Poisoned it." A finger of coldness touched Jamie's spine. He sensed what was coming. Mr. Hammond went on quietly. "You know what the poison is, without me having to name it. You know what the people round here think happened up there in the crypt. It's all come back now, all the old superstition. They're afraid, Tim. They were too frightened even to talk to the police, in case something might . . ." He shook his head, helpless. "And there's nothing I can say that can change it. They won't believe me, won't listen when I try to explain."

Stillness came, separating them from each other. Tim reached forward across it, laid his hand gently on the shoulder below him. His words faltered from him.

"It'll be OK, Grandad. They'll come round to believing you, you'll see . . . If it helps any, *I* believe you anyway."

The vicar raised his arm, without turning. He patted Tim's hand with his own.

"Thanks, Tim." He smiled. "There's hope for you yet."

And, from his place by the door, Jamie watched. He watched Tim's face, wondering. Wondering what Tim really believed. And whether there *was* any hope now, for him or for any of them.

9

_♦_

"**G**ood heavens, there can't be much more of the stuff, surely?" Mrs. Hammond paused at the window, toast-rack in hand. "I would never have believed the sky could've held all this."

From his seat by Tim at the kitchen table, Jamie followed her gaze outward. He knew what she meant. The snow must have fallen all night, was still falling now. The sky had burst open, like a pillow. The world was just feathers. In London he would have enjoyed it, but here he felt different, strangely uneasy. He wondered why.

His unease was echoed by the voice at the window: "It makes you feel so helpless, doesn't it? As if there's nothing you can do about it."

Tim answered brightly. "Well, I suppose we could try having a bit of toast to kick off with."

Mrs. Hammond looked round at him blankly for an instant, then down at the rack in her hand. She came across to the table, sighing. "The bottomless pit."

"The sky? Or my stomach?"

"Both. And go easy on the butter."

"Sorry. Where's Grandad got to? Has he had his breakfast already?"

"Yes, he was up early. It's part of his new macho image."

"OK, OK, I just overslept a bit, that's all. Where is he, anyway?"

"He's taken a few groceries and things down to Miss Dodds and Mrs. Brewer, to make sure they're all right. Old folk get a bit frightened of snow like this. It makes them feel trapped."

Trapped. That was it, Jamie thought. That was why he felt uneasy. He looked up again at the window. Beyond it the Grounds lay concealed. The snow glided down from them, moving in closer. He watched it moving, feathering the panes, thickening soundlessly flake by flake. It was the silence of it that was frightening, and the stealth; the silent stealing in against the cottage, the slow smothering. As if it knew you were here.

"D'you reckon we'll be OK, Gran? D'you reckon we ought to have another go at the lane?"

"Oh, we'll be all right, I'm sure. I should leave it if I were you, until it stops a bit."

"*If* it stops."

"Unless you want to, of course?"

"No way. Me and Jamie can hardly move after yesterday."

"You need a walk then, to get rid of the stiffness."

"Yes, we . . . we thought we'd probably go out after breakfast."

"Still, it's a good job you did it. The lane, I mean. I can't think what it'd have been like if you hadn't. At least it meant your grandad could get out to the main road."

"Is he . . . is he OK this morning?"

"Oh, he's all right, Tim, don't worry. It was just rather painful for him, going back over it all yesterday."

"We didn't ask him to. He—"

"I know you didn't. He wanted to, to help clear the air a bit. It did, didn't it?"

"Oh yes."

"And it's not just that, not just the awful business last year. It's . . . it's the village too. The way they've all taken it."

"Yes, he told us. They think it's because of the legend, don't they?" He bit his tongue. "Sorry."

"Why sorry?"

"It's a sort of promise we made to Grandad. Not to mention it to you or anything. So as not to upset you."

"Oh, that's all right. I don't mind, this once." She smiled. "Your grandad's far too concerned about other people's feelings, you know. Perhaps we're stronger than he thinks."

Tim frowned, suddenly thoughtful. "Perhaps he's the one who's not very strong, really. Perhaps he's the one who's the most upset of anybody, without really sort of knowing it."

"Yes. I think you're probably right, Tim. He's taken it badly. Oh, it's hit us all pretty hard of course, especially Alex and Mrs. Gregson. But it's been worse for your grandad than for anyone in a way. It's easy to see why, I suppose. He's put up such a fight against superstition since he came here, and now this happens and . . ." She fell silent for a moment, gazing absently down at her empty cup and turning it round and round in the saucer. She shook her head. "This old story has got a lot to answer for."

Tim glanced up sharply. "You and Grandad don't believe it, do you?"

"Oh, no. No, of course we don't. But we know its power, all the same."

"What power, Gran?"

She paused again, searching the teacup for the words which would help her explain. "Its power over people's minds, perhaps. In a place like this, old tales can seem so real if you let them. That's why their power's so dangerous. If you give them any chance at all, they've got a way of making you believe them."

"How d'you mean? I don't get you."

"Don't you? You ought to. You've seen it happen yourself. We all have. We gave the old Lychwood tale its chance, didn't we, and look what—"

"When? When did we?"

"You know when. Last year, after supper that night. Its power came from the telling of it."

"But what difference did that make? Us talking about it, I mean? It couldn't have made any difference to the . . . to what happened up at the church, could it?" He stared at her. "You don't mean we sort of *made* it happen, do you? The . . . the bell and everything?"

Mrs. Hammond set her cup down firmly in the saucer. "No. Of *course* not. I didn't mean that at all. I meant that *because* we were talking about it at the time we started making connections, and . . . Oh, I don't know, Tim, I can't explain. You've always told me I'm hopeless at explaining things. Look, I've no idea what possessed old Mr. Jefford to do what he did or what happened to him up there, but one thing I *do* know—that there must have been a perfectly rational explanation for it all which has got nothing to do with . . . with superstitious nonsense."

"What d'you reckon it was then, Gran? This explanation?"

"Probably that he was following up some new information he'd been given for that book of his and then had the most dreadful accident. Now let's get the day started, shall we, or we'll still be here at the breakfast table when your grandad comes in." She pushed back her chair and stacked up the plates on a tray.

Jamie watched her. Her hands said the same as her voice had; their briskness was final. Once she turned from the table, all talk would be over for good. He forced out his question before his last chance slipped away.

"This visitor, Mrs. Hammond . . . Was it ever found out who it was?"

"Visitor?"

"You know, the person he said was going to tell him—this new info, I mean."

"Oh, don't *you* start, Jamie. We had enough of that from the police. The answer's no, anyway. The mysterious visitor's still a mystery. Too scared to come forward probably, poor soul, after what happened. Now move yourselves. If you're still intending to fit a walk in before lunch you'd better get going. Where are you thinking of heading?"

"Oh . . . oh, just round about here really."

"Fine. Well, wrap up warm and don't get lost. If you're not back by one, I'll send Grandad out with a little barrel of brandy under his chin."

"Don't worry, Gran, we'll be back. Just save the booze till we come in, OK?"

Mrs. Hammond sighed and moved away to the sink. "I think you're turning into one of those delinquents, Tim. It's London I blame, of course. It's not safe to allow you out alone on the streets."

Behind her back, Jamie caught Tim's wink. In spite of himself, he smiled. He knew what Tim was thinking. He was wondering if she'd still feel the same about the danger of London if she knew where they were going now.

"Your gran won't be able to spot us from the kitchen, Tim, will she?"

"No way, the garden wall cuts off the view from downstairs. And even if she does we can say we were just going up to the High House."

"Why should we want to go up to the High House?"

"Oh, I don't know. To make a snowman for Alex or something. We can worry about that later, can't we? There's no point getting worked up about things that haven't even happened, is there? I'd have thought we'd got enough to worry about already, with the things that have."

"You can say that again."

"Come on then, get stuck into that other wellie and let's get moving. We're not going to solve anything just hanging around here in the porch."

"Are we going to go the same way as . . . as last time?"

"We'll have to. It'll be bad enough as it is. If we try any other route, we'll probably be buried alive in snowdrifts."

"Cheerful. OK, I'm ready."

They set off, heading upward from the cottage, following the path that they'd followed once before. They went in single file. Jamie used the tracks that Tim had left behind him, stepping high to keep the snow out of his boots. The path seemed lost now, hidden and forgotten. But it wasn't really. It was still there, somewhere deep beneath him, forcing him on blindly to the tunnel of the trees.

Tim paused and pointed forward.

"The trees, Jamie. If we make straight for them, we won't go far off course. They mark the avenue, remember?"

"Yes."

He remembered. The memory leapt up sharply, so sharply that he shivered. For an instant, night returned. He saw the yellow rings of torchlight on the avenue before him and the hard December blackness of the earth and sky beyond. And he heard too. Even sounds were clear now, voices in the silence, the words of Alex and the vicar as they'd led the way ahead. For a moment more he listened, then the memory receded. He looked about him, startled by the change. It seemed so different now, this soft and gliding whiteness. The hard black land had vanished. Only its ghost remained.

Tim's voice came backwards, breathless. "Not far now, thank goodness. My legs are killing me after yesterday."

The trees came closer and drew level, then met above them in a black-ribbed vault of snow. Tim paused again, as if unwilling to continue. He turned to Jamie, trying hard to smile.

"Brings back memories all right, doesn't it? It's only about a quarter of a mile now. We'll soon be at the rutty bit where Alex told us to watch our ankles, then we'll be out of the trees, remember?"

"As if I could ever forget. D'you reckon we'll run into Alex, Tim? Or Mrs. Gregson?"

"Not a chance. Gregson only comes up a couple of times a week now for a bit of a clean-round for Alex, and I shouldn't think she'll come in this weather. And Alex isn't in this morning either—Gran said she saw him footing it down to the village before we were up. He'll probably have lunch at the pub."

"Which way did he go, then?"

"Same way as we are, dodo."

"He can't have. We'd have seen his tracks."

"Are you joking? You can hardly even see ours."

Jamie followed Tim's eyes, back down the way they had come. The snow had come with them, creeping behind them in silence, burying all signs of their passing in soft shrouds of whiteness. No one would know they were here.

Tim turned back to the archway of beeches. "It'll ease off a bit under the trees, anyhow."

"It'll need to. Just look at us." He brushed the crust of feathery crystals off his parka and jeans. "Nobody'd ever spot us if we got lost, Tim. We look like the . . ."

"Like the what?"

"Nothing really."

"Oh come on, what were you going to say?"

Jamie bit his lip. "Like the . . . the Invisible Man."

"Oh." Tim lowered his face for a moment, then looked up with a nervous grin. "We'd better get going, hadn't we, before we give ourselves the spooks. Come on, I'll lead."

They moved forward into the tunnel of tree trunks. As the beeches thickened, the snow lost its grip on the pathway, but they could still feel its presence above them, like a gathering weight. When a wind brushed the ceiling of branches, it sifted and fell like loose plaster. Jamie spoke in a whisper, afraid that the slightest vibration might jolt it all down.

"It's dead quiet, isn't it? No wonder your gran didn't want to come up here yesterday. I don't reckon I'd fancy going inside that place on my own."

"Me neither, not even with two of us. I'm damn glad we didn't bring the keys. It'll be weird enough just seeing it from outside."

"If we *can* see it, that is—it looks as if the snow's coming on worse than ever. And I'm not so sure now what it'll prove even if we can."

"Well, it was your idea to come."

"OK, OK, I know. I just thought it'd be a good starting

point, that's all. To sort of refresh our memories or something."

"I'm beginning to wonder if I *want* mine refreshed. Anyhow, come on now we're here, and let's get it over with. It's not much farther."

They were there almost before they knew it. The last trees fell away at their backs and the snow swept towards them again like a billow. Then the church took shape. It loomed up before them, barnacled with whiteness, sudden and silent as a phantom ship. Jamie stared at it numbly, blinking the snow from his lashes, seeing the details slowly emerge. The tower, the nave, the squat little chapel . . .

Tim shivered. "Shall we . . . shall we just go as far as the west door and then call it a day?"

"OK."

"You were right when you said about refreshing our memories. It all comes back, doesn't it?"

"And how."

Jamie fell silent. It had all come back. It wasn't daylight he walked through, across to the tower. It was darkness. He heard the voices again, as he'd heard them then, the voices of Alex and the vicar; their footsteps rushing back round to the window, and the sickening rupture of glass. And his own footsteps, forcing him forward . . . For the first time since he'd left Lychwood, the image of the crypt leapt clear: the steps, the stone, and the outstretched body, the pickaxe and shovel and oblong of earth. Its vividness stunned him. He saw it all, detail by detail, the pattern of objects fixed fast in the glare of the lamp. Then he caught his breath. He'd forgotten till now that the keys . . .

Daylight returned. The image had gone now. Tim's voice was speaking, close by his ear. They had reached it already, the door to the tower.

"Well, here we are then, Jamie. There's not much to see though, is there, now we've come all this way? D'you reckon it's helped any?"

"I . . . I'm not sure really."

"They've replaced the window in the crypt, anyway. And the door, Gran said." He hesitated, then went on more firmly. "And they've put the stone back too, apparently. So it's all right now."

Jamie looked at him. "Why did you say that?"

"What? Oh . . . well, you know."

"Look, Tim . . ." Jamie waited, trying to summon the words that he knew were needed. "Look, it's not all right, is it? That's why we're here. We've got to get shot of that other idea, haven't we, if we're going to get anywhere? We've got to forget it. At least to start off with."

"What idea?"

"Oh come on, you know what I mean."

"OK, OK. It just seems different now we're here, that's all. It's all very well saying forget it, but . . ." He eyed Jamie suddenly, his voice edged with challenge. "Anyway, be honest, are you really as sure as you sound?"

"About what?"

"That the village isn't right after all?"

"Hell, Tim, how am I supposed to know? The only thing I'm sure about is that we've got to *start* as if we're sure. We've *got* to, OK?" Tim shrugged and turned away. Jamie moved nearer, put his hand on his shoulder. "Listen, Tim, it's going to be fine if we don't let ourselves get . . . get scared. We've got to stick with our original plan, like you said you wanted to down by the shop on Sunday night. And we're not doing too badly so far, are we? We've taken the first step already, if we'd only admit it."

"What step?"

"We've decided it wasn't an accident."

The words had been spoken now. Jamie felt the chill of them, creeping through his body. He shrank closer to Tim's shoulder, away from the creeping of snow. Silence came. Tim's voice hardly broke it.

"OK, Jamie. What's the next step?"

"The one we fixed on. If it wasn't an accident, we've got to assume the police were right. That it was . . . that it was murder. We've got to start off by assuming that somebody managed it somehow, even if it seems crazy. We'll just go through it bit by bit, sort of logically, OK?"

"Yes." Tim turned now, but his eyes were lowered. "Hell, I'm not being much help, am I? It's just that . . . well, it all seems so hopeless somehow. The police had a whole year and—"

"So what? They weren't here when it happened, were they?"

"How d'you mean?"

Jamie hesitated, frowning. "Well, they were working in the dark, weren't they—sort of from outside? But we were *inside*. We were here all the time. If we're right, Tim, if it was murder, there's got to be an answer somewhere, a sort of pattern. If we can just try and fit things together—"

"But what things?"

"I'm not sure. Things we've heard and seen, stuff like that."

"Heard and seen where?"

"Oh, everywhere. In the cottage, and . . . and up here. We've just got to go through it all again, and not leave a stone unturned . . ."

His own words took him by surprise. His voice trailed away. They caught each other's eye. Tim tried to grin. "I hope it won't come to that, anyway. That was only going to be our last resort, remember? You know—if all else fails."

Jamie looked at him for a moment in silence. "Yes," he said. "Well, let's hope it doesn't."

Tim's grin trembled away. "I'm beginning to hate all this, I really am. I don't see how the hell we're *ever* going to find out what happened. And I'm not even sure I *want* to anymore, are you?"

"No."

Tim's face tightened. Jamie saw the pain in it, and understood. He felt the same pain in himself. "But we've *got* to, Jamie, whether we want to or not. For . . . for Grandad."

Silence came again, and coldness. Beyond the narrow porchway the snow had thickened, moved in closer, driving them up hard against the door. Tim's edginess returned.

"This snow's beginning to give me the bloody creeeps. It's as if it's trying to scare us off. Or . . . or forcing us to go inside this damn place or something."

"Oh for God's sake, Tim, pack it in, can't you? We're scaring ourselves, that's all. I told you, if we start doing that, we've had it. It's like your gran was saying, about making connections where there aren't any—it can't scare us if we don't let it, OK? And it can't force us in there either, can it? The door's locked."

"Is it?"

"What?"

"Well, we don't know, do we? We haven't tried it."

They stood eye to eye, not speaking. A new feeling rose in Jamie, half fear, half anger, like a wave of defiance. But whether defiance of Tim, or of something else, something nameless, he couldn't be sure. "Go on then," he said. "Try it. Then we'll know."

Whatever the feeling, he saw it reflected in Tim's eyes too, as he faced him. And he heard it in the voice that answered.

"OK. I will."

Tim turned away. He paused for a moment and stared at the handle, then reached forward slowly and took a firm hold. He wrenched it upward and pushed. The door held fast. But the noise of the latch was as loud as a gunshot. It exploded the silence. They heard it leap out, in widening ripples of sound through the nave. And upward too, throbbing away through the tower. They raised their eyes, followed it, listening. For an instant it seemed to have died. Then faintly, high up above them, something responded, catching its echo, suddenly stirring awake. They knew what it was they were hearing. A tiny pulsation of iron.

Tim jerked back from the handle. His face was like death.

"It's . . . it's going to ring! God, let's get the hell out of here!"

They ran, out into the swirling churchyard, and the whiteness swallowed them up.

The thing they'd awoken settled back down into darkness. Their footsteps were buried behind them in the gathering silence of snow.

10

◆

"**W**hat a lousy wash-out."

Tim spoke to himself, not needing an answer. He sat hunched on the edge of his bed after lunch, and stared down at nothing. From the edge of his own bed Jamie looked up for a moment, wondering what he could say that would bridge the short distance between them. But he couldn't find words that would reach even that far. He shrugged and was silent.

He remembered the words Mrs. Hammond had spoken at breakfast. *Old tales can seem so real if you let them. That's why their power's so dangerous.* And other words too. Tim's words this morning. *Be honest, are you really as sure as you sound? That the village isn't right after all?* He shivered, driving the tale from his mind. They had to forget it, pretend that they didn't believe it, and try to start somehow all over again.

"Tim . . ."

Tim answered without looking up. "What?"

"Aren't we going to do anything?"

"I thought we already had."

"I mean this afternoon. And anyway, can't we just forget all that?"

"Some hope."

"OK, so we scared ourselves half crazy. Big deal. But nothing really happened, did it?"

"You're damn right it didn't. The whole morning got us precisely nowhere."

"You know what I mean. I don't reckon it was as much of a wash-out as all that, anyhow." He frowned, remembering. "It sort of brought things back a bit."

"It did that all right."

"Well, at least that was something. It was a hell of a sight better than what we're doing now."

"So what d'you suggest?"

"I told you, we've got to do what we fixed on. We've got to assume the police were right, and just go through it all logically."

Tim sighed. "OK. Where do we start?"

However grudging they sounded, Tim's words were enough. Jamie sat forward. "We start with all the people involved. It's not that wide a field, is it, from what we've heard about the keys? Apart from Old Jefford, the only people who could've known where to find them were the Committee. So, just supposing Old Jefford didn't take them himself, one of them must have. And they all had the chance, didn't they? They were all in the dining room from six till seven. Agreed so far?"

"Uh-huh."

"Oh come on, Tim. You were dead keen on the idea when we got here. Have you lost interest or what?"

"Of course I haven't. It's just that it suddenly seems so crazy somehow, thinking that one of them could have—"

"Too bad. It's no good if we start getting wet about it. We've got to look at it like a math problem or something."

"Oh great. It should be a brilliant success then, where I'm concerned."

Jamie ignored him. "So we'll start at the beginning and go through them one at a time. You know—motives and alibis and everything. We'd better kick off with your gran and grandad."

"*What?*"

"Look, it's only a process of elimination, isn't it?"

"Oh give over, can't you? How could—"

"We've *got* to do it this way, Tim. It's only to clear the decks a bit."

"Are you out of your mind or what? Gran and Grandad?"

Jamie clenched his teeth, biting back the anger that was going to come. "OK, let's leave them out of it and push on, then. The next one's Alex—"

"*Alex?*"

"Oh for God's sake, Tim!"

"Well, how can it have been Alex for crying out loud?"

"I'm not saying it *was*, am I? I'm just trying to narrow it down if you'd only shut it for a minute and listen."

"OK, keep your hair on. I'm listening, aren't I?"

Jamie glared at him in silence, then braced himself for one final effort. "All right. Alex is the one who picks up all the loot apart from Mrs. Gregson's ten thousand, and he gets the High House thrown in as well. So, as far as I can see, he's got the best motive, hasn't he?"

"Oh brilliant. So it was Alex, then. On to the next case."

"Hell, Tim, you don't even try, do you?"

"Well, it's barmy going through all this. I mean, he's got the best alibi too, hasn't he? He was with us in the sitting room the whole time, in case you'd forgotten, wolfing down scrambled eggs on toast."

"He went to the john on his own, didn't he?"

"Oh magic. What's he supposed to have done? Nipped out of the window and up to the church with his fly open?"

"Oh stuff it! I'm going downstairs." Jamie leapt to his feet and moved swiftly across to the door. Even before he could reach for the handle, Tim was beside him, his hand on his arm.

"Jamie—"

"Stuff it, I said. You asked me to help and I was trying to, that's all. But if you want to pack it all in, that's OK by me."

"I *don't*."

"You could've fooled me. Everything I say, you just—"

"Look, I'm sorry, OK? It's . . . it's because of this morning, that's all."

"What about this morning? I told you—nothing happened, did it?"

"It's not that."

"Well, what then?"

"Oh, I don't know. I can't explain."

"Suit yourself." Jamie shrugged him aside, reached down again to the handle. He didn't turn it. But this time it wasn't Tim's hand that stopped him; it was his voice.

"OK, Jamie, if you want to know. I'll tell you. It's because I feel a bloody failure."

The voice was quiet, but Jamie heard the pain in it, the same pain he'd heard this morning, up by the church. He paused again, fumbling for words.

"It wasn't just you, Tim, was it? You weren't the only one who got scared. It was me too, wasn't it?"

"It's not the same. Can't you understand?"

Jamie understood. He didn't need to ask what Tim meant,

or who it was that he'd failed. He turned now, to face him, but his eyes were still lowered.

"Look, I know it's not the same, Tim, but . . . well, if it makes any difference . . . I'm pretty fond of him too."

Silence came between them. For a moment their eyes didn't meet. Then Tim drew a breath, and smiled.

"Thanks," he said.

"That's OK."

For a few seconds longer they stood there, not speaking. Then Tim swung away and plummeted back on his bed. When his voice came again, all earlier shadows had left it. "Anyway," he said, "if we're going to get this thing figured out, it's about time we did something useful."

"You don't say? Got any brilliant ideas, then?"

"I have, actually. It's just come to me."

"Another Norfolk miracle. Go on then, shoot. I can't wait."

"Hard luck, you're going to have to. Till tomorrow morning at any rate. But if it's facts about the Church Committee suspects we need, it'll be worth it. It's perfect."

"Uh-huh. What's the catch?"

"Only catch-22. No spadework, no supper."

"What? Oh God, Tim, not the lane again?"

"Not the lane, no. But you're still going to need some real muscle-power for the next two or three days. It's going to be the new macho image from now on."

"I thought as much. Go on, explain."

Tim went on, and explained.

"Come on, you two, you've done enough. You must be frozen. How about a cup of something to warm you up before you go back? That's the least I can do."

Tim caught Jamie's eye. He drove the spade down hard into the high bank of snow that they'd shifted aside from the pathway. "Oh, great," he said, "we'd love to. Thanks very much."

Shoulder to shoulder they took their boots off on the doormat, and stepped forward into the house. Mrs. Poole closed the door behind them.

"I *am* grateful to you both, I really am."

"Oh, that's OK."

They sat opposite her at the kitchen table, warming their hands on the mugs. She was elderly, but not like Mrs. Hammond: less soft, more smartly upright and severe. Jamie wondered if she'd once been a headmistress. It was her hair that made him think it, raked back in a bun as if she wanted it kept strictly in its place. But a few strands had escaped and dangled loose across her forehead. They made him feel less nervous. A headmistress who had slightly lost control.

"You'll have to make do with my company, I'm afraid— Edward's appointments aren't over for another three quarters of an hour or so yet. He always goes on till twelve thirty on Wednesdays."

"Oh, really?"

"But he'll be so pleased when he sees the wonderful job you've done. It was so kind of you to offer."

Jamie felt his first pang of guilt. He glanced away from her eyes, round the kitchen. It was far bigger than he'd expected, and far more beautiful. At least two rooms, he thought, knocked together into one, and every wall and recess was gleaming with antiques. And the smells were the same, smells of oldness and comfort. Lavender and spices. But somewhere, faintly, another smell lurked, a sharp white odor that didn't belong. He frowned, trying to place it.

"Do you like it, Jamie?"

"Sorry?"

"I said, do you like it? The kitchen?"

"Oh. Oh yes, it's great. It must be fantastic to have all this space. Mum'd love it."

"Yes, it's convenient—especially for Edward, with the office just through the door there behind you."

The office . . . That was it. The words brought the smell out of hiding, gave it a name. Ether. He'd smelt it before, in the hospital room where his grandad had died. The kitchen was just like it, the same strange mixture. Lavender and ether. Like a sickroom full of flowers . . .

He thrust the thought from him. "It's much bigger than I thought it'd be, Mrs. Poole. I hadn't realized it was all one cottage. It looks like two from outside."

"It used to be, when we first came here. But we've been very lucky. We managed to buy up the adjoining one when it came up for sale about five years ago, and knock them both together."

"You've got some amazing stuff here."

"Yes, it's been great fun collecting it all. We've picked up most of it since we extended, to fill up the space. And we built the new office on at the same time, so it's been a pretty chaotic few years. Still, it's nice getting things as you want them at last, I must say—although I almost feel guilty about it sometimes. A place this size for just the two of us, I mean."

Jamie didn't answer. He held his breath, waiting. Beneath the table a foot had tapped his own, twice against the ankle. The signal they'd agreed on. Tim had seen the opening that he'd hoped for. He was ready with his bait.

"Oh, I shouldn't worry, Mrs. Poole. Crumbs, look at the High House. It's vast. And before Alex came, Mr. Jefford was there on his own."

The line spun out towards her. For an instant she looked

wary, and circled it in silence. Then she turned and snapped it up.

"Yes, poor Mr. Jefford . . . such a terrible business."

Tim knew that he had hooked her. "You can say that again. It was about the most awful night me and Jamie've ever been through."

"I can imagine. I was so upset, to think of you both in the middle of it all like that. It was bad enough for poor Edward, even, getting dragged into it as he was—not that I'm blaming your grandad for calling him, I didn't mean that. It was the only thing he could have done under the circumstances."

"It was lucky he *was* dragged in. I don't reckon Grandad could've coped without him."

"Well, thank heaven Edward was at home when he called, then. It was a near thing—he hadn't long been back from visiting a patient. And I don't know what I'd have done if he hadn't been here, I'm sure. Still, it's behind us now, at least."

"Yes, I suppose so. But I don't reckon Gran and Grandad have really got over it yet. Especially Grandad. He's still pretty cut up."

"I know. He was always so kind to Mr. Jefford, and far closer to him than anyone else in Lychwood, apart from Alex and Mrs. Gregson."

"Didn't you know him very well, then? You and Dr. Poole?"

For the first time, Jamie thought he caught a tiny hesitation in her voice before she answered. But her words had swept it from him before he could be sure.

"Oh, not really. Not in the past five years, anyway. Since his sister-in-law died, that is."

"His sister-in-law? I didn't know he had one."

"Well, of course. Alex's grandmother. Alex didn't see much of her himself, while his firm was down in Exeter, but old Mr. Jefford was terribly attached to her. All the more so, probably, because he'd never had a wife of his own. Her death came as the most awful blow to him. She was the only family he'd got left, really, and she'd been living with him for quite a few years—"

"Living with him? Here in Lychwood?"

"Oh yes. Up at the High House. She'd been a widow for quite a time, and she came to Lychwood when her son and daughter-in-law—Alex's parents, that is—were killed in a plane crash."

"But you said she only died five years ago. I've been coming up here for longer than that and I never set eyes on her. I'm sure I'd have remembered if I had."

"Oh, that's not really so surprising, Tim. She didn't go out at all towards the end. She was far too ill for that. You'd have liked her, though. She was a lovely old thing."

"Did you see a lot of her, then?"

"Quite a bit. At least Edward did—he was their doctor, you see, hers and Mr. Jefford's, so he looked after her right through her last illness. She thought the world of him. I think that was why . . ."

She bit back the words she had almost spoken. They watched her, wondering why she had stopped.

"Why what, Mrs. Poole?"

"Oh . . ." She shifted. Her eyes shied away from their own for a moment, down to the lap of her skirt. "Nothing really. I was just going to say that that was why we were both so sorry when she died, that's all." She looked up again, smiling. But behind the smile a shadow had come, watchful and wary.

Tim had seen it. He avoided it, changing his tack.

"It's dead weird to think of Mr. Jefford being fond of anybody. I thought that book of his was the only thing he really cared about. It's a bit sad in a way, isn't it, to think it'll never be finished now, after all the work he did on it?"

"I suppose so. But I doubt he'd have found a publisher for it, even if he *had* finished it. It wouldn't have been of much interest to anybody outside Lychwood, I shouldn't think. And even here in the village there are lots of people who mightn't have taken too kindly to it, having him discussing their houses and everything in print. Heaven knows what he might have said."

"I know what you mean. I suppose they mightn't have bothered so much about being written about if Mr. Jefford had been a bit more . . . well, friendly or something. I mean, if he'd tried to get on with them a bit more. Not that I really knew him of course." He glanced up from his mug. "What *was* he like, Mrs. Poole?"

Her smile came again. But the shadow was still there behind it. Jamie could see it, sharp and dark at the back of her eyes, like a shutter about to fall.

"Oh, it's not for me to sit in judgment, now that the poor man's dead. Let's just say that he wasn't always the pleasantest of people to deal with, shall we? He was too vindictive, and . . . and fanciful."

"Fanciful? How d'you mean?"

The shutter fell, sealing the answer away behind it, out of their reach. She shrugged. "Oh, I can't explain. And it's of no importance now, anyway. So, how's that coffee going?"

"Oh, fine. Nearly finished. We'll have to be off in a minute, anyhow, or Gran'll start getting panicky about lunch. Still, it's been really great—being able to chat it over, I mean. It's sort of put my mind at rest."

"Oh? In what way?"

"Well . . ." His gaze fixed on her for an instant. He lowered his voice. "Actually, Mrs. Poole . . . we haven't breathed a word to Gran and Grandad or anything, but . . . well, me and Jamie've been feeling dead scared."

She responded at once, curious and concerned. "Scared, Tim? Of what?"

"Oh . . . of that old legend, I suppose."

There was a moment's pause. When she finally answered, her voice had tightened. "Oh *that*. Put it out of your heads. Or, better still, talk to your grandad—he'll tell you what he thinks of it. It's only a pity the rest of the village aren't as rational."

"So you think it was . . . you think the police were right, then?"

"What?" She bridled suddenly. "No, of *course* I don't! It was a horrible accident, that's all, whatever the police may think. Edward's said so all along. Not that anything he said made any difference. They wouldn't take a blind bit of notice of what he told them even though he was the first to examine the body, a good hour before they'd arrived."

Jamie remembered. The image rose up, superimposed on the kitchen. The daylight receded, replaced by the glare of the camp-light, and he stood once again by the door of the crypt. Below him lay pickaxe and shovel, the dust-shrouded body, the keys at its shoulder, the oblong of earth at its feet. And, beside it, the doctor. Alone there, crouched at the end of his own web of shadow, his fingers exploring the folds of dead cloth.

Mrs. Poole's face returned, and her voice, still speaking. "It was so unfair of them. Calling his professional judgment in question like that. And that wasn't all. What upset him most was the way they laid into him for other things, when the suspicion hadn't even crossed his mind that—"

"What other things, Mrs. Poole?"

No answer came. The stream of her words froze abruptly. Jamie's attention sharpened, focusing on her face. But her eyes didn't see him. They were flickering past him, beyond his shoulder, across to the door at his back. Perhaps she had felt she'd said too much already. Or perhaps . . . His heart missed a beat. In spite of himself he glanced round behind him, half expecting to see a familiar form. But he didn't. The door wasn't open. Only a thin gust of ether met him. But stronger now, colder, scalpel-sharp.

Mrs. Poole's voice recalled him.

"What's the matter, Jamie?"

"What? Oh, nothing. I just thought I heard something, that's all."

"It was only Edward, I expect, in the office. Anyway, come on, both of you. This won't do."

She rose now, gathering up the mugs. The gesture was brisk: it was time the discussion was closed. And yet, somehow, her face didn't show the same briskness. Her eyes looked uneasy. As if there was something she wanted to settle, but wasn't quite sure how to say.

It came at the door, at the very last moment, when she'd thanked them again for their help with the snow.

"Enjoy your last few days in Lychwood, won't you? And if I were you I'd put all that other business out of your heads. It was just a very sad accident, that's all, and best not talked about too much. I'm glad it's been helpful, chatting it over and everything, but I'm sure the most sensible thing now would be to . . . to forget we ever mentioned it. At least promise me you'll try to, anyway."

Tim grinned. "Try anything once, that's what I say. Thanks for the coffee, Mrs. Poole, it was great."

The front door closed behind them. Their eyes met for an instant but they turned away, not speaking. They set off slowly homeward, up the pathway through the garden, past the newly-built extension where the office was housed. The place was quiet. All the patients must have gone now. But behind his frosted window Dr. Poole would still be there. They glanced at it in passing, then went on again in silence, as if some instinct warned them not to put their thoughts in words. The glass looked blind enough from outside. But from inside . . . They weren't certain. Perhaps, beyond the blindness, there were eyes that watched them go.

11

⸻ ◆ ⸻

The double ringing came again, shrill and urgent from the hallway. Tim and Jamie looked across the table at the vicar, expecting him to leave the dining room at once. But he made no move to go.

"It's for you, Tim," he said.

"What?" Tim glanced away towards the door then back towards his grandad. "What d'you mean?"

"I'm not sure I can make it much clearer, really."

"But how d'you know it's for me?"

"He rang just before you got back this morning. I told him to phone again at one-fifteen."

"It's not Dad, is it?"

"No. Local."

"*Local*? Who is it?"

"There's a pretty obvious way of finding out, I'd have thought. But you better get a move on or you'll miss your chance."

Tim left his seat, still frowning, and hurried from the room. The ringing ceased abruptly. His voice replaced it, at the far end of the hall.

Jamie tried to listen. A numbing thought had touched him. Perhaps the call was linked in some way with this morning. Perhaps the doctor . . . He strained his ears. But through the thickness of the wall and door Tim's words were only echoes, too shadowy to hear.

"Come on, Jamie, eat up. You can finish off the custard if you like."

"Sorry?"

"The custard." Mrs. Hammond smiled and pushed the jug towards him. "Tim'll put you out of your misery in a minute. The call's for both of you really."

The thought returned, more numbing than before. "Both of us?"

"Don't worry, it's not bad news. Unless you've got major plans for this afternoon, that is. Have you got anything fixed?"

"Well, sort of . . . We sort of thought we might do a bit more snow-clearing round the village or something."

"Good heavens, I'd have thought you had enough of that to be going on with. You're supposed to be on vacation, aren't you? Who were you thinking of digging out this time?"

"Well . . ." He bit his lip. "We thought somebody in one of those little places down the road might need a bit of a hand perhaps . . ."

But he was spared from further detail of the "somebody" they'd fixed on, whose image had been haunting him throughout the whole of lunch. The door was thrown open. Tim rejoined them with a grin.

"Hey great, Jamie. Change of plan. Three guesses who that was."

"How should I know who it was?" But at least Tim's face had told him who it wasn't. He felt himself relax. "Can't you just tell me?"

"Alex."

"Alex? What did he want?"

"We've got an invite for this afternoon, you and me. He's offered to stand us another tea down at the Bakehouse, like last year."

"Hey, brilliant."

"Anyway, you might've *told* me it was Alex, Grandad. I felt a real cretin out there, not knowing."

"I'd have thought you could've worked it out for yourself."

"Some hope. I didn't even know he'd got a phone, did I? He hadn't last year."

"Oh, there've been quite a few changes up at the High House since then." He rolled up his napkin and pushed his chair back sharply from the table, as if to thrust aside all mention of the past. "Come on, put paid to that custard and let's hit the washing-up. What time are you meeting?"

"Quarter to four, he said. He's going to get there first, to bag a table by the window."

"Fine. I should take things easy till then if I were you, and leave the Good Samaritan bit till tomorrow morning. By the look of the sky the snow'll still be there, and more. Come to think of it, you'll probably find yourselves back at the Pooles' place before you know where you are, starting all over again. Seems to me your good works could land you in quite a vicious circle if you don't watch out."

Tim chuckled. "Could be. I just hope it's not too vicious, that's all. But don't worry, we'll watch out all right. Won't we, Jamie?"

Jamie smiled back. "You bet," he said. But behind his smile he felt suddenly cold.

The coldness grew worse. It moved against them as they turned out of the lane into the roadway, stinging through their parkas and jeans. Dusk had crept in early, and settled in the hollows of the snow.

The lights were on already in the windows. Jamie glanced at them in passing. The Wilkies'. Mrs. Gregson's. And the Pooles'. All here, then. All assembled. Three lights against the darkness. And one of them could lead him to the answer to a death. Unless . . . He shivered slightly, hunching up his body to protect it from the cold. Unless the answer was elsewhere, outside, here in the darkness. Perhaps the darkness was the answer. Perhaps the villagers were right. He edged closer to Tim's shoulder. The touch awoke Tim from his thoughts.

"What d'you reckon, Jamie? D'you reckon we ought to ask him straight out?"

"Ask who?"

"Well, Alex of course. D'you reckon we ought to come straight out with questions?"

"I suppose we haven't got much option. As long as we don't sound too keen, that's all."

"I don't see how we're supposed to ask things as if we don't want to know the answers. Come to that, I'm not sure what we're supposed to be asking anyway."

"We've just got to try and fill in the gaps in her story. Mrs. Poole's, I mean. I reckon the bits she didn't give us are just as juicy as the bits she did."

"Suppose so. But how d'you ask questions about things somebody *didn't* say? If there *were* things she didn't say, that is. Hell, Jamie, we might just've been imagining it, mightn't we?"

"No."

"D'you reckon she gave us any clues, then?"

"Plenty, I'd have thought. Or, at least, plenty of things that need checking up on."

"Search me if I know what they are."

"Well, for a kick-off, who this patient was that Doc Poole's supposed to have visited after the Church Committee meeting."

"We can't ask Alex that. And he probably wouldn't know anyway."

"I didn't say he would, did I? I just said it was one of the things we've got to check up on."

"I don't see how."

"Nor do I yet. Still, there are loads of other things."

"Such as?"

"Look, Tim, I thought the idea was that we were going to do our own thing, sort of follow our own leads till we're dead sure we're right. So as not to put each other on the wrong track or anything."

"I suppose so."

"Well, it was your idea."

"OK, OK. I just seem to be on about twenty tracks at the moment, that's all, all going in different directions. That's the trouble, if you ask me. Every time you get a new angle, about another twenty crop up you'd never even thought of before. It could go on forever. How are we supposed to know what's important and what's not? No wonder the police packed it in."

"Hell, we haven't even started yet. We can't solve anything till we've got the facts worked out, can we?"

"OK, you don't have to tell me—it's like a math problem. Which probably means that Hammond's going to make one almighty cock-up of it, like he always does. I reckon there's something wrong with my brain, actually. Math makes it sort of seize up. I told old Creepy Crawley that after our last test."

"What did he say?"

"He told me I ought to get on to a doc quick, before finals." He chuckled suddenly. "Perhaps I ought to see Doc Poole about it. From what Mrs. Poole said, Old Jefford and this sister-in-law used to rate him as the world's number one genius."

"Used to."

"What?"

"Used to. Before Old Jefford packed him in."

"What're you on about?"

"You told me yourself last year, dodo. Old Jefford was the only bloke in Lychwood who ended up not using him. You said he went to some private doc in Norwich. I wonder why."

"Hey, I'd completely—"

"Like I said, the juicy bits are the ones people don't let on about. So let's hope Alex will. Here's the Bakehouse."

"Hey, hang on a minute—"

"Too late. There he is. He's seen us."

Alex was waving. He had managed to get them the table right next to the window, and even before they had joined him Jamie could see just how much he had changed. The same change he'd seen in the face of the vicar, the same rings of darkness that hollowed his eyes. His hair and his features had thinned. He ordered the tea, and his talk seemed as cheerful as ever. But Jamie was sure that the cheerfulness cost him an effort. Beneath it, the pain of last year had dug deep.

They chatted their way through a mound of hot teacakes, avoiding the shadow that hovered behind every word. And, in spite of his earlier plan to ask questions, Jamie felt glad to avoid it, at least for a while. He sat back in his chair, relaxed in the warmth of the Bakehouse, and listened to Tim rattle on about London and school. It was good to relax, a relief in a way to pretend for a time that last year hadn't happened. And it was so easy, here, to pretend. With its smells of warm bread and its everyday bustle, the Bakehouse was somehow a place set apart. It seemed too far removed to be touched by the darkness, too bright and lively for shadows of death. But he knew he was wrong. It was no good pretending. He turned his head slightly, away from the table. Outside the window, the night had closed in.

Alex leaned over towards him and looked past his shoulder out into the gloom.

"What's up, Jamie?"

"What?"

"You looked as if you'd seen a bogey out there or something."

"Oh . . . no, sorry, Alex. I was just seeing if it was snowing again."

"God, I hope not. The High House is nearly marooned as it is. If we get any more of the stuff, I'll have to call on your professional services."

Tim glanced up sharply. "Come again, Alex?"

"This charity you're supposed to be running. Spade-Aid, or whatever it is. I hear you've been digging out the Pooles . . . Sorry, have I said something I shouldn't have? It's not supposed to be hush-hush, is it?"

"Oh, no . . . no, course it's not. We just didn't reckon it'd have got round yet, that's all. We only did it this morning. How did you hear?"

"Village hot line." Alex laughed. "Good heavens, Tim, you've been up here often enough to know what Lychwood's like. You can't scratch your armpit up here without hitting the headlines."

"That's what I told Jamie last year—gossip's the only hobby they've got round here. Still, I wouldn't have reckoned they were so hard up for thrills that they'd get turned on by a bit of snow-clearing."

"You're dead right, there. You'd have thought they'd had all the thrills they needed in the past twelve months."

"Oh, I didn't mean . . ." Tim faltered, suddenly crimson.

"I know you didn't, you idiot." Alex laughed again, in an awkward attempt to put Tim at his ease. But the effort rang hollow. "Anyhow, it's pretty hopeless trying to avoid the subject, isn't it, after all you both went through?" He lowered his eyes, as embarrassed as Tim. "That's partly what this tea's for, really. A feeble sort of 'sorry' or 'thanks.' Something like that, anyway."

"Crumbs, Alex, there's nothing to say sorry about. You needn't have, honestly. Bought us tea and everything, I mean."

There was a long moment's silence. Then Alex glanced up. His awkwardness still hadn't left him, but this time his laugh was sincere.

"Hell, you might've told me that before eating it all, then, and saved me two quid." The tension broke. The sounds of the Bakehouse leapt vividly back into focus. "Come on, let's talk about it a bit, shall we? It'll do us all good."

They talked about it. And, as they talked, Jamie relived it, instant by instant. Old shadows emerged, summoned out into the open, and he felt the old chill of them, creeping its way up his back. But he knew that it wasn't just these things that chilled him. There was something far closer, a still darker shadow, that moved him more deeply than those of the past, in the face here before him. It made him aware how much Alex had suffered. His face was as gray as if shadowed with pain.

The minutes ticked by. Their words flowed more freely. They went through it all from beginning to end. Then a hush fell between them. They slipped into silence, as if they had foundered in thoughts of their own. It was Tim who first broke it.

"What do *you* reckon happened, Alex? *Really* happened, I mean?"

Alex sighed. "I don't know, Tim. I've been over and over it till it's driven me half crazy. But I just don't know. The verdict the police came up with doesn't seem to make much sense at all. I honestly reckon they thought there was somebody else in that damned place all along, and that we were just too blind or too half-witted to spot them."

"But there *wasn't* anybody. There couldn't have been. There's not even a pillar or anything they could've hidden themselves behind. I saw every inch of the place when I looked in from outside, even the corners under the window. So did Jamie."

"So where does that leave us?"

"Well, if it *was* . . . if it *was* murder, whoever it was must've got out somehow after they'd done it."

"No, the police ruled that clean out. And considering the hours they spent in there I'm prepared to go along with them, at least that far. The door was locked all right, and the keys by Uncle's body were the ones that locked it, there's apparently no doubt about that."

"What about a secret tunnel or something?"

"Oh, you can forget about the storybook stuff. The cops wouldn't have missed a trick like that. They went over the place for a month with a fine-tooth comb. They weren't born yesterday. And anyway, it still doesn't answer the craziest question of all: what was Uncle doing there in the first place? What could have persuaded him to go there on a filthy cold night in the middle of winter? And *why*, for crying out loud? If somebody wanted to . . . to finish him off, why couldn't they have done it up at the House?"

Jamie looked up thoughtfully. "Perhaps it was a blind. A sort of cover-up. Alex, this visitor . . . Who d'you reckon it was?"

"Beats me, Jamie. The police gave everybody in Lychwood third-degree treatment, I can tell you, especially the immediate locals."

Tim broke in quickly. "What made them lay into Doc Poole like they did, Alex?"

"Who told you that?"

"Oh—I'm not sure, really. Grandad, I think."

"It wasn't anything serious. Or, at least, not anything that seems to have much bearing on the case, as far as I can make out. It was just that he allowed half the village to traipse round the so-called scene of the crime when he ought to have known better. Though how he was expected to have 'known better' when he hadn't even so much as suspected foul play's a mystery to me. Anyway, he wasn't the only one who got it in the neck. We all did."

"But still they didn't get any leads on this visitor business?"

"No, Jamie, not a dickey-bird. Whoever it was is sitting pretty tight—if there *was* anybody at all, that is. We don't even know if they ever turned up."

Tim frowned. "But if they didn't, why should your uncle have gone to the church?"

"Exactly. Like I said, the whole thing just goes round and round in crazy circles. All I know for sure is what I told your grandad—that Uncle was hoping for some kind of meeting that night, before he came down to the cottage."

Tim fidgeted nervously with his empty cup. "It's so weird.

I mean, how could whoever it was be so sure your uncle wouldn't tell you or Mrs. Gregson about it? If he'd told you the name of who was coming, this visitor would've been in a pretty tight corner, I'd have thought."

"It must have been someone who knew him too well, I suppose. Someone who knew how much he enjoyed keeping secrets up his sleeve, at least where I was concerned. All points to someone in our little Lychwood circle, doesn't it?"

Jamie shivered slightly. When he spoke, his throat felt dry.

"Alex, what did your uncle say exactly, when he mentioned this meeting?"

"I told you, he'd got hold of some info about this legend—"

"No, I mean *exactly*. The exact words. What you told us in the sitting room that night, remember?"

"God, Jamie, that was ages ago." His brow puckered in thought. "I think it was: *I'm hoping for a meeting which'll settle it one way or the other*. Oh, I don't know, something like that. Does it matter what—"

"A meeting . . . So he mightn't have actually said it was a visitor, then? I mean, he mightn't have used that word?"

"Well, I'm not certain . . . But no, I don't think he did, anyway. It comes to the same thing though, doesn't it?"

"I . . . I'm not sure."

"Jamie, are you OK?"

"What?"

"Are you OK? You're not cold, are you?"

"No . . . no, I'm fine." Beneath the table he clenched his hands, as if in an effort to steady his voice. "Alex, do you believe in the legend?"

The words dropped into silence, as heavy as stones. For

a moment, Alex seemed hardly to gather their meaning. Then he sank back in his chair, and pressed both his hands to his eyes.

"I don't know anymore, Jamie. I honestly don't know. I sometimes think it's no less crazy than any other explanation. Perhaps it's the only one that makes any damned sense at all." His hand fell away. He saw their faces. "Hell, I'm sorry, I didn't mean that, I really didn't. Just forget it, OK? It was a bloody stupid thing to have said." He looked suddenly, indescribably weary.

Tim bit his lip. "It's us who should be sorry, Alex. It can't be much fun for you, going back over it all like this."

"Oh, that's OK. It was my idea anyway, wasn't it? Like I said, in a funny sort of way it helps."

"Look, don't worry. I bet it was an accident all along. Gran and Grandad think it was, anyhow."

"Yes. They're fantastic people, Tim, you know that?"

"Yes. I know."

"And it's probably about time you headed back in their direction. They'll be wondering where you've got to. It's gone five already. Miss Merrett's got her eye on us, you know—it's about time we cleared out and let her get on with the washing-up."

Jamie looked round, startled. Alex was right. The Bakehouse was almost empty.

"Thanks for the tea, Alex. It's been great. And . . . and thanks for talking to us."

"My pleasure, Tim. I told you, it helps. And we've just about run the subject dry, haven't we?"

Tim hesitated. "Well . . . sort of . . ."

"I don't believe it. There can't be anything else, can there?"

"Oh, not really anything important. Just something me

and Jamie were wondering about, something we sort of heard." Tim faltered again. His eyes met with Jamie's, then awkwardly darted away.

Alex looked from one to the other, clearly bewildered. "Well, come on then. If there's something you think I can tell you, spit it out. But I don't promise to have any answers." Footsteps moved through the Bakehouse, across to the door. The final two customers left. "Come on, Tim, or we're going to get ourselves thrown out. Two questions maximum, OK? Then we'll call it a day."

"OK . . . It probably sounds a bit weird, really, but . . . well, we sort of heard that your uncle used to think Doc Poole was a really great bloke, and so did your gran—"

"My gran?"

"Yes, when she was up at the High House. When she was ill. Before she died, that is . . ."

Alex looked more bewildered than ever. "OK, right so far. So what's the question?"

Tim hung back for an instant, then took the last plunge. "Well, why did your uncle stop using him after your gran died? Why did he go to some Norwich bloke instead?"

"Good heavens, what makes you ask that?"

"Oh . . . nothing really. I told you, it was just something we heard. I suppose it's a bit personal . . ."

Alex shrugged. "Not really. It's pretty common knowledge round here, anyway. There's not much that isn't. And Uncle certainly wasn't one to keep his opinions to himself, especially when he got one of his cracked ideas."

"Cracked ideas?"

"Oh yes, he had plenty. This particular one was a bit strong, though, even for him."

"What was it?"

"Just that he accused Doc Poole of gross incompetence.

He held him totally responsible for my dear gran's death."

They stared at him, speechless. Behind them, Miss Merrett was clearing the counter. Alex held up his hand for the bill. Then he turned back to face them, and smiled.

"Time's about up. If you've got one last question, you'd better make it pretty sharpish."

Tim opened his mouth, but Jamie's voice checked him before he could speak.

"Alex—five years ago. Did Doc Poole win the jackpot on the slots or something?"

"What on earth—"

"Five years ago. When they built the new office and bought a second cottage and stuffed the whole works full of antiques—"

For a moment Alex seemed too stunned to answer. Then, for the first time in an hour, the shadow lifted from his face. He laughed aloud as if refreshed.

"Good God, Jamie, talk about village gossip. You beat the lot of them. You're wrong on one point, though. It wasn't the slot machines that coughed up the jackpot for old Doc Poole. It was Gran. She willed him half her fortune for all his tender care. A hundred and twenty thousand quid."

12

♦

"**I**'m not exactly looking forward to this, Tim."

"Joe's out, anyway. His van's not here. So at least it's going according to plan so far."

"Big deal. I'm still not looking forward to it."

"We mightn't get asked in, anyhow. Even if he does do us the favor of letting us clear his snow for him, we probably won't get any tea or coffee or anything for it."

"Yuk. I'm not sure I'd want it. The place looks as grotty as hell."

"Well, it's our only chance of talking to him, so we'd better make the most of it. Here's the gate."

"You could've fooled me. It hasn't got any hinges, has it?"

"'Fraid not. It's pretty classy string, though." Tim paused for a moment with the string in his hand, and looked Jamie straight in the eye. "Anyway, why not admit it?"

"Admit what?"

"It's not the grot that's bugging you, is it? It's the thought of Old Wilkie. You're just dead scared."

"Oh, brilliant. So what's new? He gives me the spooks, that's all."

"Join the club." Tim grinned, but Jamie saw the nervousness behind it. "Still, Gran reckons he's pretty harmless. He's just a bit gaga."

"I'm not sure."

"Oh well, here goes. Let's get it over with, shall we? The front door's round the side."

They edged through the gate and closed it behind them as well as they could, propping it against its single post. Then they made their way up to the house.

"God, what's under all these tarpaulin things, Tim? It looks like a scrap heap or something."

"It is. Bits of old tractors and cars and things. Joe picks it up."

"What for? Repair jobs?"

"Some of it is, for people round the village. It brings him in a bit of extra loot, I suppose. He's always dead hard up, I told you."

"What about all the rest of the junk?"

"Oh, that's just for fun. He's brilliant with engines and stuff like that. He built that van of his from scratch. I helped him a bit with the electrics the summer before last."

"This place must look one hell of a mess in summer."

"You can say that again. Grandad calls it the iron boneyard."

The iron bones were shrouded now, in shapeless mounds of snow. But here and there the shrouds had sagged and shifted and the loose skin of tarpaulins showed through gray. Jamie hurried on between them, after Tim.

The pathway led up round the corner of the cottage. When they reached the door Tim halted and cursed beneath his breath.

"What's up, Tim?"

"It's pretty obvious, I'd have thought. The snow round here's been cleared already. Joe must've done it earlier this morning."

"So what do we do now?"

"Search me. There might be some more round the back that needs doing, I suppose. What d'you reckon? Or shall we pack it in and go and try the next job on our list?"

"Suits me. This place gives me the creeps."

"He mightn't be in, anyway." Tim's voice dropped to a whisper. "I can't hear anything in there, can you?"

They listened. The cottage was engulfed in silent whiteness. It seemed to hold its breath and listen back.

Even Tim's low whisper echoed loudly. "We've got to do something one way or the other. We can't just hang around out here all day . . . Oh what the hell, let's give it a try."

They moved together, up onto the doorstep. Tim raised his arm to knock. But his fingers never reached the rusty knocker; his hand froze in mid-air. As if aware of what it was he wanted, the door had clicked ajar. Jamie found himself confronted by a sudden crack of darkness. A face appeared within it, on a level with his own.

Old Wilkie looked at him, not speaking. His face seemed still more shrunken than when Jamie had first seen it, but its movement and expression were the same. The same lopsided wagging, the half-closed eye that watched him, the smile that knew more secrets than it told. The silence lengthened. The head ticked out the seconds, one by one.

It was Tim who was the first to find his voice.

"Hello, Mr. Wilkie, we're sorry to disturb you and everything but we thought . . . well, we've been doing a bit of snow-clearing round the village, and we thought you might need a hand or something. Only it looks as if . . ."

His voice trailed away. Old Wilkie's eye had shifted, and caught him in its beam. He spoke now.

"You've come, then. I knew."

"Well, we just thought—"

"I knew. It'd be sooner or later, I said. I been waiting."

"Oh. Great. Well, if you've got any spades or anything—"

"Joe's done that."

"Oh, I see. It's just that we thought there might be some more. Round the back or something—"

"Ay, Joe's done that. It's not the snow you're wanting. You come in."

The face disappeared. The dark crack of the doorway widened. A breath of stale hotness gusted from the sitting room beyond. Jamie turned and caught Tim's eye. Tim looked badly frightened. He started as the face appeared again.

"You coming, then? Let the heat out."

For a moment more they waited, glancing at each other as if afraid to move. Then, before he could be sure how it had happened, Jamie found himself with Tim inside the house. The front door closed behind them. With a bony rattle, curtain-rings clattered on a pole.

"Keep the draft out."

Old Wilkie's hand had dragged a drape across the doorway. Their only means of exit had disappeared from view.

He turned to face them now, his head still wagging. The same words came again.

"You've come, then."

Tim swallowed. "Yes, but . . . but we can't stay long, Mr. Wilkie."

"It'd be sooner or later. I knew."

"How . . . I mean, how did you know? We—"

"I been watching." His smile grew more crooked, up the left half of his face. His eye was only wrinkles.

"Watching?"

"Seen you, I have. Yesterday and Tuesday. You come with me."

They recoiled slightly as he pushed his way between them, across the tiny sitting room towards a second door. When he reached it he turned round again and beckoned. They followed.

They found themselves inside the kitchen of the cottage, even smaller and more stifling than the sitting room they'd left. The air was too thick to inhale here, and clogged with smells of deep-frying. But it wasn't only these things that made Jamie catch his breath. It was the windows. One on each side of the kitchen. Old Wilkie pointed, grinning, to the right and left in turn.

"Yesterday. And Tuesday. Out there."

Jamie followed the direction of the finger. He felt his stomach sink. The right-hand window looked towards the village. Not fifty meters distant was the office extension; and beyond it, with the spades they'd used still upright in the snowbank, the path they'd helped to clear for Mrs. Poole. And the left-hand window . . . He knew before he turned his head what view he'd see out there. The same view as the one from their own bedroom, the pathway leading upward and the snow-enveloped tower. But even clearer from this angle. If eyes had been observing from this window—Old Wilkie nodded on, as if in silent confirmation. Every move they'd made on Tuesday had been watched.

Then the silence was broken. A wheezing sound was coming from Old Wilkie, from somewhere deep inside him.

And Jamie knew what he was hearing, even though the sound was voiceless and the face had shown no change. It was laughter.

The laughter turned to coughing. Then Old Wilkie spoke again.

"No. It's not the snow you're wanting. You go and sit down. There's a bit of fire in there, and a nice drop of tea soon."

He moved towards the cooker. They watched him for a moment as he fumbled with the matches. A hissing filled the kitchen, then exploded into life beneath the kettle. They turned away and left him there alone.

The sitting room was far too cramped to leave much space for comfort; the only chairs it offered were the two beside the fire. They sat in them and waited, and listened to the sounds beyond the doorway. The water rose to boiling; a whistle screamed and died. Jamie looked across at Tim in desperation, but Tim just shrugged his shoulders. He was right too, Jamie thought. They'd got only what they'd asked for. It was this that they'd been wanting, not the snow.

The footsteps shuffled back towards them. When Old Wilkie entered, he was carrying enamel mugs of tea.

Tim leapt up from his armchair.

"D'you want to sit here, Mr. Wilkie? We couldn't see any other—"

"You stay put. I like the fireplace. Here, nice drop of tea for you."

"Great."

"You drink that down you."

Jamie drank as best he could. The tea was dark and sickly sweet, and bore the taint of something rancid. The handle of the mug was slick with fat. Old Wilkie squatted close between them, on the cross-bar of the fireplace, with his back towards the narrow iron grate. He sipped his tea, not speaking, and rocked his body gently, as if he had forgotten they were there.

Then suddenly his eye jerked up towards them. He turned and leered at each of them in turn.

"Ay, I knew you'd come. I knew you couldn't leave be."

Tim fought to find his voice. "Honest, Mr. Wilkie, we *would've* cleared the—"

"Honest, is it?" The eye caught him again. "There's folks that may be, and folks that mayn't. That's what Lychwood is. And no way of knowing." He spoke like Joe, in disconnected fragments. But between the spoken fragments little ghosts of meaning hovered and seemed to give half-glimpses of the thoughts inside his head. "Think you know, do you? Think you're clever?"

"Well, no . . . I—"

Old Wilkie's body swiveled. The eye lurched round to Jamie. With a tightening of his stomach Jamie shrank back in his chair. Suddenly the old man's hand came forward, and stopped within a foot of Jamie's face. Between the thumb and forefinger it held a silver coin.

"Know what this is, do you?"

"Yes. It's a . . ." Jamie faltered into numbness. He stared, not at the coin, but at the fingernails that held it. They were horny as a badger's, and embedded thick with dirt. "It's a five-pence piece, Mr. Wilkie."

"Ay, a shilling, that's what it is. You want it, do you?"

"Sorry?"

"You want it? You just hold your hand out. You catch it when it drops."

Helpless, Jamie did as he was ordered. Old Wilkie's fist closed slowly on the coin, six inches above Jamie's upturned palm. Then the fingers spread and opened. But Jamie's palm stayed empty. The coin had disappeared.

Old Wilkie slumped back. They heard his voiceless laughter.

"Think you're clever, do you? Think things are what they look like? Like those policemen, you are. No time for magic, policemen."

Tim sat slightly forward. His eyes had come alive now, but his face was deathly white.

"Magic, Mr. Wilkie?"

"Ay, magic. Wouldn't understand that, not policemen. Lock people up, they do, instead."

The heat had grown intense now, from the nearness of the fireplace, but Jamie felt a coldness in his spine. It wasn't just the strangeness of Old Wilkie's words that chilled him, it was something in the expression of the old man's face. The leering made it difficult to know what he was thinking, like a mask which hid the workings of his mind.

"What magic, Mr. Wilkie?" Tim said. "Conjuring tricks, d'you mean?"

"Maybe I do. And maybe I don't." He squinted up at Tim. "Don't know the difference then, that it? Not so clever now, are you? Not with all your London schools and books and learning. Same as *he* wasn't, with all his. Got what was coming, in the end."

Tim stiffened. "You mean . . . Mr. Jefford?"

"Naming no names, I'm not. The one you come about, that's who I mean. Not the snow."

"Did you . . . did you know him very well, then?"

"Ay, knew him all right we did, me and Joe. Knew Lord High and Mighty. Not so High and Mighty now though, down there in St. Andrew's. Don't need Wilkies any more to do his digging. Do his own digging he can now, down there. Grow his own daffydils." Deep inside him, laughter wheezed again.

Tim clutched his mug, white-knuckled, and waited for the spasm to subside. "Digging, Mr. Wilkie? You mean you and Joe used to *garden* for him? Up at the High House?"

"Didn't know that then, eh? Not so sharp as you thought, are you? Ay, all the mucky jobs for Wilkies, up at the High and Mighty High House. Muck, the Wilkies are. Told you that, haven't they? Folks round here?"

"No, course not. Who—"

"Nice clean churchy folks. Committee folks." His wagging face crept closer up to Tim's, so close that Jamie held his breath. "Told you about their own muck too, have they? Too la-di-da for that, were they, with their money and their nice big houses? Forgot to tell you where it come from?"

"Who d'you mean, Mr. Wilkie?" Tim braced himself, and swallowed back his fear. "D'you mean the Pooles?"

"Might be them. Might be others." The hand pounced up. Tim's head recoiled. The forefinger and thumb which gripped the coin had almost touched his face. "Might be folks that's got big houses that their husbands bought 'em. Folks whose husbands . . ." He didn't voice the ending. His fingers voiced it for him. They closed, then sprang wide open. The silver coin had vanished into air.

Old Wilkie sank back. His grin fell raggedly apart.

"Forgot to tell you that, did they? About how they got their nice big houses, thieving other people's money? Wouldn't call it thieving, though, not them. Wilkies though—that's different."

The eye left theirs and gazed down at the hearth-rug. He rocked himself in silence. His face had changed, as if the mask had sagged and darkened. Then he spoke, like some-one speaking to himself.

"Didn't do it, though. Not Joe. Not thieving. He's a good boy, Joe is."

Tim glanced across at Jamie. "Thieving, Mr. Wilkie?"

"Not him. Wouldn't do that, not Joe. Got money enough of his own, Joe had, without thieving from the likes of him. Lord High and Mighty Jefford."

"You mean . . ." Tim stared. "You mean Mr. Jefford accused him—accused Joe—of . . ."

"Glad to go, we were. Good riddance. A wrong 'un, he was, with his books and la-di-da. Got what was coming to him, though. Do his own digging now, he can, down there."

His voice fell silent. Behind his back the fire slumped and shifted. A coal clattered out into the hearth. Jamie jumped as violently as if the sound had burnt him. And somewhere deep inside him a memory awoke. The memory of a paper in a little pool of lamplight, a paper which had blown from the surface of a desk. The last word to be written by a man whom death had silenced. He remembered how he'd stood there, with Tim's hand on his shoulder; he remembered Tim's voice asking if anything was wrong. And there *had* been something wrong, there'd been something on that paper . . . Then the noise had come, as now, the crash of something falling. But that time it had been a falling log—

Tim edged slowly forward in his armchair, as if afraid to wake Old Wilkie from his thoughts.

"Mr. Wilkie . . . What d'you reckon happened that night? When that bell up there rang?"

Old Wilkie gazed on down into the hearth-rug. "Didn't hear no bell, me and Joe. Having our supper we were, with the telly. Good boy, Joe is, always gets me supper. Heard the crash, though. Later, when they found him. Come up then, we did. Not so High and Mighty then, he wasn't, lying there."

When Tim spoke, his voice was hardly louder than a whisper. "Do you . . . do you know who did it, Mr. Wilkie?"

In the silence, the old head nodded on. But whether he was answering, or dreaming, was impossible to tell.

"Do you, Mr. Wilkie? Please tell us."

The answer came at last. "Might've been any."

"Any?"

"Always been like that, it has, up here. From the beginning. Might've been any. And never a way of knowing which one's next."

"I don't get you, Mr. Wilkie. You mean you don't know—"

"Never a way of knowing, not when it comes."

"When what comes?"

"Might've been any. You or me."

"What?"

Suddenly, Old Wilkie's eye awoke. Jamie's heart leapt to his throat. It was as if a presence had awoken in the room. The air was charged with it, like something that was going to explode. And he heard it in the words the old man spoke now. But whether it was fear or whether threat he couldn't tell.

"It's come back."

"What?"

"It's come back. Like it's always done."

"What has? What's come back, Mr. Wilkie?"

"Waited its chance, it has, and come back. And never a way of knowing which one's next. Don't understand that, though, policemen. Don't understand magic. Lock people up, they do, instead . . . You go now!" His voice rasped out, loud and sudden in the stillness of the cottage. The old mask of a face was wagging faster. They scrambled to their feet. "You forget it. Leave it be. You go back home now!" He struggled up.

"It's OK, we're on our way. Thanks for the tea and everything. We—"

"You go back home!"

"We are, OK? Gran's waiting, anyway—"

"No, you go home. Back to London."

"What? We can't do that! Not till Monday—"

"You go to London!"

They hurried to the door. Tim's hand wrenched back the curtain and fumbled for the latch. A fist of icy air struck in against their faces.

"You leave it! You leave it be!"

Then the door had slammed them out into the cold.

13

Tim's edginess had grown. On the morning following their visit to Old Wilkie Jamie trudged along beside him, down the lane towards the high street, and watched him kicking grimly at the snow. Another inch had fallen in the night. He gazed around him, where the white land led away. But there was no land now, and no leading. Only empty whiteness, as dimensionless as space.

"At least the snow's stopped, Tim."

"You'd better keep your voice down. It'll hear you."

He knew what Tim was feeling, although neither of them spoke it. The sky was thickly laden. It hung heavy, gray as iron, like a dead weight close above them. But it wasn't dead; just waiting, and gathering in silence. Its silence wasn't deadness, but a holding of the breath.

"You OK, Tim?"

"What?"

"You OK? You're not saying much."

"Oh, I'm just knackered, that's all, after last night."

"Well, it was you who wanted to stay up and see the New Year in. Your gran—"

"OK, OK, I know. Anyway, it's not just that. It's . . . it's yesterday morning as well."

Jamie didn't answer, or need to be reminded. He could see Old Wilkie's cottage on the far side of the road. And the sense of fear or menace hadn't lifted since he'd left it. It had spread now. It was out here, in the sky.

They reached the ending of the lane, where it opened on the roadway, and paused there for a moment as if unwilling to go on. Tim didn't look at Jamie. With lowered eyes, he watched his bootcap furrow idly at the snow.

"Oh, what's the use, Jamie?"

"What's that supposed to mean?"

"You know what it means. It means we're not getting *anywhere*. Well, are we?"

"Not standing here, we're not. And anyway, it's not true. We've come one hell of a way since Sunday."

"OK, so maybe we have. But it's *Friday*. We've been at it for *five* days."

"So what?"

"Oh come on, you know what. We've got to spend this afternoon with Gran and Grandad, haven't we? It'd really hurt them if we missed Gran's New Year tea. And that only leaves us two full days after today."

"Fine. We're supposed to be tackling Gregson at the moment, aren't we, not hanging round here."

"OK, so we go and see her. And where's that supposed to get us?"

"I don't know, do I? But we're not going to find out if we don't go."

"I suppose so. It's just such a lousy muddle, that's all. All this new stuff we keep hearing about people. And there doesn't seem a hope in hell of finding out if it's important or not. Even if Gregson doesn't let on about this disappearing husband of hers, she'll probably come up with a whole load of other things that'll all need checking out."

"OK, so we'll check them out. That's what we're here for, isn't it?"

"But when, for God's sake? We've only got —"

"Look, we'll manage, OK? Like we've managed so far. We've done a pretty good job on the Doc Poole info, haven't we? At least we know now that he *did* see a patient that night."

"It was only a fluke, Gran coming out with that."

"So what's wrong with flukes? It's still info, isn't it? At least it's fixed now that he was down with Mrs. Brewer from eight ten till about eight thirty-five. *She's* not likely to be lying, is she?"

"But it still doesn't tell us the main thing, does it? We still don't know what he was doing at eight o'clock, do we? There's only Mrs. Poole's word for it that he was at home till eight ten. He could easily have got back down to Mrs. Brewer's place in ten minutes if he was up at . . . at the crypt." He shivered suddenly, and hugged himself more tightly from the cold. "Oh forget it, Jamie. I'm sorry, OK? We've done all right. It's just . . . well, yesterday morning, that's all. It really spooked me up. And I'm not even sure where it got us."

Jamie didn't answer for a moment. He turned his head and gazed across the road towards the cottage, three hundred meters distant. From here, the place seemed silent; the hedge concealed the windows. But he moved in close to Tim and dropped his voice.

"Tim, you remember when we were up at the High House last year? You know, when we —"

"Yes, OK, I know." Tim spoke quickly, as if to thrust the memory aside.

"Well, you remember that sheet of paper I was looking at when you came down from upstairs, the one Old—"

"What of it?"

"Nothing struck you as weird about it, did it?"

"Weird? What d'you mean, weird?"

"I . . . I'm not sure. It came back to me yesterday, that's all, the feeling I'd had when I was looking at it. As if there was something on it that was . . . well, sort of wrong. Or creepy or something. But I can't recall—"

"Look, Jamie, do we have to? There wasn't anything, honestly, I'm dead sure there wasn't. It was just some stuff about the cottages down here, that's all. I even tried to get Mrs. Poole talking about it, remember? But it didn't seem to lead anywhere."

Jamie frowned. "D'you recall exactly what it said? I mean—"

"No, of course I don't, not exactly. But it was only history stuff. Dates and things, and architecture. The only creepy bit about it was that it was the last thing he ever wrote before he . . . well, you know. So let's drop it, Jamie, OK?"

Jamie dropped it, and let his thoughts drift outward with his eyes, back towards Old Wilkie's cottage.

"Tim . . . what did you really make of it? All that stuff he was on about?"

Tim glanced up. "Who?" Jamie's eyes were still turned from him. He followed their direction. "Oh." He hesitated, suddenly uneasy, as if to put his thoughts in words might make them real. "I though we were supposed to be sort of doing our own thing. You know—following our own leads and that kind of stuff, so as not to put each other on the wrong—"

"I know. I just thought perhaps this might be a bit different. Like Alex said and everything—talking might sort of help."

Tim looked away, back down at the furrow his boot was scooping from the snow. "Yes. Yes, OK. I don't mind . . . Which bit did you want to talk about?"

"Well, all that stuff about magic, I suppose, and . . . and something coming back. And about 'it could've been any of us.' What d'you make of it?"

Tim's uneasiness increased. His eyes darted to and fro across the roadway. "Well . . . it could've been three things really, I suppose, as far as I can see. It could've been what I said before we got there, only worse than I reckoned. I mean, he could be a real head-case, completely cracked. Or . . . or it could be that he's pretty sure the legend's true, couldn't it? He might really believe there's something up there, and was trying to warn us to steer clear. He might've meant that it got Old Jefford because he was fooling about up there, but that it . . . it could've got any of us. Or . . ."

"Go on, Tim. What's the third idea?"

"Well, perhaps he was doing it deliberately. You know—just putting it on. To sort of scare us off."

"But why should he want to?"

"Search me. It doesn't make much sense, really. And it doesn't seem to get us any further, does it, whichever of the three it was?"

"I'm not sure . . . But there's a fourth possibility too, isn't there? One that sort of includes all your three?"

"A fourth one? What?"

"Well, what if he believes that this thing, this magic or whatever it is, this power—"

"This what?"

"Power. You remember? It was in that old priest's day-book, about God departing and another power entering in and . . . well, taking possession."

"I . . . I don't get you."

"Well, perhaps he thinks that this power *has* entered in and kind of taken possession."

"Possession? What sort of possession? Of the church, d'you mean?"

"No. Not just the church. I mean possession of *him*." Jamie drew a long breath. "Perhaps he reckons he's possessed."

Tim stared. His lips looked blue with cold. "But . . . but why, for God's sake? What'd make him think that?"

"Don't you see, Tim? He might think it could've been any of us, but it chose *him*. And he couldn't resist it sort of taking him over. You remember what he said about the police? Perhaps he meant they wouldn't understand, they'd just lock him up instead."

"They wouldn't understand what? Jamie?"

"Well, that it was this power that had taken him over and . . . and made him do what it wanted. Made him . . . murder."

He stopped speaking, and dropped his gaze from Tim's. He realized suddenly that they were both trembling. They stood there for a while, their eyes not meeting. But the silence of the snow was worse than words.

"Come on, Tim, we ought to be heading for Mrs. Gregson's. I'm frozen."

"Yes. OK." But Tim made no move to go. "Jamie, d'you really believe that—about what you were saying?"

"Oh, I don't know. It's just the only thing that seems to make any sense out of all the garbage he was talking, that's all. Unless . . ."

"Unless what?"

"Unless your first theory's right." He tried to smile. "It

probably is, anyway. He's probably just a head case . . . Look, Tim, there's one way of finding out, isn't there?"

"Is there?"

"We can try pumping Joe."

"Joe?"

"Well, Old Wilkie said they were having supper in front of the telly at eight o'clock, didn't he? If Joe goes along with it, it'll just about louse up my theory, won't it?"

"Hey!" For the first time, Tim's face brightened. "That's right! Look, I reckon I can handle Joe OK. I'll try and catch him tomorrow when he's out in the van or something. It should be dead easy to get him talking. And that'd as good as put Old Wilkie in the clear, wouldn't it?"

"Sure . . . Come on, let's get moving, shall we?"

They set off side by side along the road to Mrs. Gregson's. Jamie watched him as they went, from the corner of his eye. The change was almost startling: Tim's darker mood had lifted. It was just as if the thought that Joe might wreck the latest theory, had somehow proved a positive relief. As if . . . Jamie walked in silence. It was his own mood, now, that darkened. He wondered how afraid Tim was of finding the solution. And he knew that he was now afraid himself.

Jamie studied Mrs. Gregson from the sofa.

He hadn't seen her for a year, not since the Church Committee meeting, when she'd come into the hallway to collect her hat and coat. He recalled his first impression: the bulk of her proportions, and the darkness of her clothing. She was still in black today, and looked as powerful as ever; but perhaps he had been wrong when he'd thought she'd looked unfriendly. He listened to the way she spoke to Tim.

"There's more tea in the pot if you want it."

"D'you reckon I ought to? I've had three already."

"That's up to you."

Unmotherly, unsmiling. But not frosty. Simply blunt. As outspoken as if Tim had been an adult.

His thoughts were brought up sharply. The talk had changed direction. And Tim was looking startled, as if he'd just been caught off guard. He'd been aiming slowly round towards the subject of Old Jefford. But she'd reached the target first; she'd fired a question out, point-blank.

"You've got over last year, have you?"

"What?"

"Last year. That business up in the crypt."

"Oh . . . Oh, yes. Well, sort of . . ."

"I'm not so sure your grandfather has. He's been looking off-color. And Alex Jefford's not much better."

"Yes, it's the shock, probably—"

"It was a shock to all of us. I've done what I can for him, of course—Alex, that is—but there's a limit."

"You still go up there then, do you? To the High House, I mean?"

"Not as much as I did. I've told him I'm happy to clean round once a week on Fridays and do some baking for him on Sunday afternoons, but he can't expect me to be at his beck and call. I've got my own life to lead. All things considered, he can count himself lucky I used to do as much as I did. His great-uncle wasn't the easiest of people by a long chalk."

"You . . . you knew Mr. Jefford pretty well, then?"

"Better than most. The Lychwood people hadn't got much time for him on the whole." She leaned forward brusquely and refilled her cup. Jamie watched her. The brusqueness might simply have been an attempt at concealment. A concealment of what, though? Affection, perhaps? A genuine fondness for old Mr. Jefford? A reluctance to show her distress at his death? He remembered the words Mrs. Hammond had spoken: *It's hit us all hard, especially Alex and poor Mrs. Gregson.* Perhaps . . . But he couldn't be sure. She sat back, and stirred her tea smartly. "He'd only got himself to blame, of course. You can't expect people to bother themselves with you if you don't make an effort to be civil."

"He was fond of his sister-in-law though, wasn't he?"

"Elizabeth? Oh, very. Probably because she was the only one who was prepared to put up with all his tantrums and nonsense. *I* wouldn't have stood for it for a minute, I can tell you that much. She was too patient by half, even when she was ill."

"What did she die of, Mrs. Gregson?"

"Weak heart, as far as I know."

"Mr. Jefford must've really missed her after she died."

"Oh yes. He went downhill badly after that." She shook her head, disapproving. "I knew he would, of course. He was always one to let his bitterness get the better of him. Even when she was alive he'd been too much of a recluse for his own good, in my opinion, but that was nothing to the way he behaved after her death. He hardly set foot outside the House."

"He did used to come and play cards with Gran and Grandad on Mondays."

Mrs. Gregson snorted. "That was about the sum total of it. Spent the rest of his time cooped up indoors with old history books. It wasn't healthy. What with that and his deafness, he was getting cut off from the world. I told Alex Jefford as much when he came here to live with him, but there wasn't a lot *he* could do, I suppose. He persuaded his uncle to let him drive him in to Norwich a few times, but even that was a battle. Old George Jefford didn't hold with cars any more than he held with telephones or anything else to do with the present. He preferred shutting himself in and digging up the past." Jamie felt his flesh crawl. The last words were startlingly vivid. He wondered whether she'd used them on purpose, but her eyes gave no clue to her thoughts. "His stubbornness proved his undoing in the end, of course. If he'd let Alex come back after the Committee meeting and drive him down to the cottage, none of it might have happened."

Tim leaned forward slightly. "Was there any sign that anything *was* going to happen, d'you reckon? I mean—"

"No, of course not. It was a perfectly normal evening— if you could call *any* evening up at that place normal, that is. It was the same routine it always was."

"What *was* the routine, Mrs. Gregson?"

She glanced at him sharply. "You're beginning to sound like a policeman."

"What? Oh, sorry, I was just—"

"You were just wondering." Her eyes remained fixed on his own for an instant, then suddenly loosened their hold. She looked back at her teacup and shrugged. "There's not very much to tell, from my point of view at least. I was in the kitchen at the back of the House, waiting for Alex to come home from the office. He always gave me a shout when he got in, before he went up to shower and change, and then I'd bring tea into the sitting room for him and his uncle and leave them to it."

"That was when Mr. Jefford told him about this visitor he was expecting, was it?"

"Presumably. I didn't eavesdrop, if that's what you mean."

"Oh . . . no, I—"

"They weren't long together, anyway. What with the traffic from Wells, Alex wasn't in until five and he had to be down at your grandfather's by five thirty or so for the pre-Committee session they always had. I cleared the tea things when he'd gone, and had a few words with Mr. Jefford about meals for the following day."

"Did he give you any details about this meeting he was expecting?"

"Certainly not. He wasn't the kind to discuss his personal affairs with me or anyone else, with the possible exception of your grandfather. I'm surprised he even gave any hint of it to Alex. I left him writing at his desk in the sitting room at just gone quarter to six, and that was the last I saw of him."

She set her cup down on the table beside her. Her face seemed to darken.

"Did you . . . did you lock up, Mrs. Gregson?"

She looked at Tim blankly, as if for a moment her thoughts had been drifting. But her voice when she answered was crisp.

"Lock up? Of course. Mr. Jefford was nervous of burglars, especially with his deafness. I'd checked the bolts on the back doors as I always did. And I locked the front door behind me when I left."

"And you didn't see any sign of . . . of anybody as you came down to the Committee meeting?"

"Not that I was aware of. Considering that I hadn't heard about the possibility of a visitor at that stage, I wasn't paying much attention. I had enough to do keeping my footing on that path down through the Grounds. You seem to have forgotten it was dark."

Jamie hadn't forgotten. Even as she'd spoken, he'd seen her in his mind's eye, moving slowly downward through the shadow of the trees. He thrust the image from him.

"And later on, Mrs. Gregson?" he said. "I mean, when

you left the cottage after the Committee meeting? You didn't catch sight of anybody then, either?"

"As far as I could see, there wasn't a soul out of doors, which was hardly surprising under the circumstances, I'd have thought—it was a bitterly cold night. Edward Poole and old Mr. Wilkie followed me out of the lane, but apart from them, Lychwood was like a ghost-town."

Her final words met with no answer from Jamie. He felt the effect of them crawl through his scalp.

"You saw them, then?" Tim said. "Dr. Poole and Mr. Wilkie, I mean?"

"Well, of course I saw them. They were coming down the road behind me by the time I reached home." She eyed him with sudden interest, as if a new thought had struck her. "I hear they've had the benefit of your services too."

"What? Oh, yes. At least, Doc Poole has. Joe had done most of the snow-clearing round at their place by the time we got there."

"Yes. Joe Wilkie's not as bad as he's painted, in my opinion. He's got his good points. There aren't many who'd look after their fathers like he does, whatever people say."

Tim paused, as if bracing himself. "Yes, we sort of heard about . . . well, about Joe. The rumors and everything."

"What rumors?"

"Oh, well, only one rumor really. But it's probably not true or anything—"

"Thieving from Mr. Jefford, you mean?"

"What?" Tim was taken aback. "Well . . . yes—"

"Lychwood gossip. No truth in it at all, as likely as not. Just another of George Jefford's fancies. One does best to close one's ears to that sort of thing in villages. It's only a pity the Wilkies can't forget about it themselves and let bygones be bygones."

"They haven't been back gardening up at the High House then, since Mr. Jefford died?"

"Far too proud for that. Alex Jefford's done his best to make amends but he hasn't met with much success so far." Her bulk shifted forward. She held out her hand for their cups. "Anyway, there's hardly any point in dwelling on all that now."

For a moment it seemed as if she was drawing their talk to a close. Tim was quick to forestall her.

"So you don't reckon there *was* anybody on their way up to the High House that night, then? To visit Mr. Jefford, I mean?"

"No. I told you. If anyone turned up at all, there was certainly no sign of them that I saw when I came away from the meeting at seven. I wasn't aware of anything out of the ordinary until the noise up at the church."

"The . . . the bell, d'you mean?"

"What? Oh—no, that wouldn't have carried this far. And I was in the kitchen anyway, with the radio on. No, I mean the din you made breaking into the crypt. I felt the impact of it even from here."

"Did you . . . did you guess where it came from, Mrs. Gregson? The crash?"

"Not at first. I thought it had come from the High House. It sounded like something exploding." She didn't look up. They watched her reliving the moment. "I left straight away, when I heard it. By the time I got to the gate to the Grounds, up by your cottage, there were more people heading the same way. The Fentons and Reeds, Mrs. Poole and the Markhams, and Joe with his father. I waited for them to catch up, to see if they knew more than I did. But everyone seemed at a loss. Then your grandmother heard us and came to the door of the cottage. She told us the few facts she'd learnt from the vicar: something had happened to old Mr. Jefford; not in the High House, but up in the crypt. I knew then." She paused, still gazing downward and slowly revolving the cup in her hands. "Yes. I knew then. I knew what had happened up there."

They stared at her, stunned into silence. As if unaware of the shock that she'd caused them, she slipped into silence herself. The room was quite still now. Only the teacup continued its movement, turned round and round by her slow, heavy hands.

"How . . . how did you know, Mrs. Gregson?"

Tim's voice was low, but it seemed to recall her. She looked at them both as if slightly surprised.

"What makes you ask that? You know as well as I do." Jamie knew what was coming. He felt his blood freeze. But it wasn't the words that she spoke now which numbed him. It was hearing the tone which she used to express them: the old tone of bluntness, as brusque and as matter-of-fact as before. And it made the words chillingly real. "You know what happened up there. You saw for yourselves what he'd done. And there seems little point now trying to find out who visited him and persuaded him to do it. The fact remains that he *did* do it. He moved the stone. And he paid the price."

14

◆

"**W**here on earth can Tim have got to?" Mrs. Hammond looked round towards the window, with her palm against the teapot. "I'll have to make a fresh cup. This is nearly cold."

"Oh, he'll be all right, Joyce."

"But it's quarter to five. It doesn't take three quarters of an hour to fetch a carton of milk."

"He's met somebody, I expect. Don't worry, he'll be back in a minute."

"Well, I hope so."

Jamie followed the direction of her eyes. The window of the sitting room was gathering with darkness. The light had lost its strength now. The panes were almost blind. A whole day since they'd talked with Mrs. Gregson. Saturday was ending. By this same time on Monday, they'd be home.

She turned back towards the fireplace and shrugged.

"Do you want any more cake, Jamie? It's another couple of hours till supper."

"I'm OK for a bit, thanks, Mrs. Hammond. Perhaps I'll have another slice with Tim."

"Yes." She sat there for a moment, still cradling the teapot. Her thoughts were written clearly in the shadows on her face. Then another thought seemed suddenly to strike her and bring a further clouding of unease. She looked across again at Jamie. "You'll be all right tomorrow, won't you, you and Tim?"

"Tomorrow?"

"You haven't forgotten, have you? David's been asked to say Evensong over in Blakeney, and we're supposed to be having tea out there first."

"Oh . . . oh, no, I hadn't forgotten. That's OK."

"It seems such a pity on your last day, but I don't see how we can get out of it now. We accepted the invitation ages ago. You really *can* come with us if you'd like to. I'm sure they'd make you welcome."

The vicar glanced up from his paper. "I should think that's the last thing they'd want, Joyce. Especially on their last day."

"We'll be fine, Mrs. Hammond, honestly."

"Oh well, if you're sure. We won't be going ourselves if the snow comes again tonight. And I don't like the look of the sky, I must say."

"Is . . . is Blakeney far?"

"Oh, not too far. It's only up along the coast road. We should be back by nine or so if—"

She started suddenly. Then the tension left her body. The front door of the cottage had been opened, and footsteps came towards them down the hall. Tim hurried in to join them. His face was raw and marbled from the cold.

"Is there any tea left? I'm frozen."

"I'll have to make another pot, I should think. This must be stewed by now."

"Oh, don't worry, it'll be fine. I like it strong. Here's the milk, anyway." He threw himself down by the fireside, next to Jamie's armchair.

"Where on earth have you been, Tim? I was worried."

"Oh sorry, Gran. I ran into Joe, that's all. We got chatting a bit."

"What about?"

"Don't ask him, Joyce, for heaven's sake. It's bound to have been carburetors and sump-oil."

Tim didn't raise his eyes. "Something like that." He leaned across in front of Jamie and helped himself to cake. As he did so, Jamie felt a crumpled slip of paper thrust quickly in his fingers. "The van seems in good nick, anyway. Joe's reckoning on driving round to Yarmouth for the day to-morrow, so he must be pretty confident."

"Isn't he worried about the snow?"

"Doesn't seem to be. The coast road's been cleared now, he said. And he reckons it's too cold for the next lot to drop yet."

Taking care to keep Tim's paper well concealed from the Hammonds, Jamie spread it slowly open on the cushion of his chair. The words were scrawled in ink: *Checked out. O.W. OK. Telly supper with J at 8.* For a moment he looked thoughtful, as if the message had surprised him. He glanced across at Tim to catch his eye. But Tim avoided contact. And perhaps it was as well to take no chances. There'd be time for talking later, when they both went up to bed. Tonight, up in the bedroom, he'd tell Tim about the talk he'd had just now, out in the kitchen, and the piece of information Mrs. Hammond had let slip. Until then they must be careful . . . He cast his eye once more across the paper in his fingers. Then he screwed it up and tossed it in the fire.

Mrs. Hammond was still speaking, with the same note of unease.

"Are you sure you're all right, Tim?"

"Sorry?"

"You looked chilled through."

"Oh, no—I'm OK. I think I'm just a bit done in, that's all. It's probably all that snow-clearing or something."

"Well, you can both have an early night. *I'm* going to anyway, with Blakeney tomorrow."

Tim's attention sharpened. "Oh . . . oh yes. What time d'you reckon to be off?"

"About three, I should think, if we're going to be there for tea. I'll leave you some soup or something to keep you going till we get back, and there'll be plenty of cold meat left over from lunch."

"Fine."

"And if we get a good night tonight, we can stay up a bit later tomorrow. We'll probably be back soon after nine, so I can do us a really nice last supper."

Behind his paper, Mr. Hammond chuckled. "I shouldn't put it quite like that, Joyce."

"What?"

" 'Last Supper.' Makes it sound a bit final."

"Oh." She looked back down at Tim and tried to smile. But her smile went unnoticed. Tim's eyes were on his plate now. His grip on it had tightened, and his knuckles had turned white.

"What?" Tim sat on Jamie's bedside, huddled in a dressing gown and blanket. The torchlight scooped deep shadows in the whiteness of his face. "Gran told you she *spoke* to her? To *Gregson?"*

"That's what she said. She's not likely to have made a mistake, is she?"

The shadows sharpened as Tim frowned. "She must have. It wouldn't make any sense at all otherwise. It'd mean the whole Committee was—look, go through it again."

"Hell, Tim, I've been through it already." Jamie bit back his increasing desperation. "OK. Gregson must've seen our torches from her window at about ten past eight or so, right, when we were heading up for the church? And she started wondering what was going on, so she rang up here. And your gran palmed her off with some yarn about your grandad deciding to go up to the High House and walk back down with Old Jefford for bridge, because the path was slippery and everything."

"So you really reckon Gran spoke to her at about ten past eight?"

"I'm only telling you what she said."

"But that's crazy. I mean, there doesn't seem a chance that she could've got back down to her own place from up there in ten minutes. And she'd have run into us on the path, wouldn't she? We left here at about five past."

"She could've cut across the Grounds some other way, I suppose."

"Not a hope. There's loads of brambles and things all over the place. And it was as dark as hell."

"She might've been ringing from somewhere else—"

"Oh, come off it. I haven't exactly noticed any phone boxes up in the Grounds. And there isn't even anything up at the High House. So it virtually sews up her alibi, doesn't it? And where does that leave us?"

"Look, we'd better keep the noise down a bit, hadn't we? It's gone eleven. Your gran and grandad'll hear us if we don't watch out."

Tim glanced towards the wall and dropped his voice. "I'll tell you where it leaves us. No-bloody-where."

"Oh, come on, Tim—"

"Well, does it? Look, what've we got? When the bell rang at eight o'clock, Doc Poole was supposed to be at home, preparing to head down to old Mrs. Brewer's for ten past. Gregson was probably down at her place, and by ten past she was phoning Gran. Old Wilkie was having supper with Joe in front of the telly. And we were down here listening to Grandad telling us that horror-story, while all the time it was . . . it was happening up there for real."

His eyes flickered over to the window. In spite of himself, Jamie turned his head and followed their direction. Beyond the pool of torchlight, the bedroom was in darkness. The curtains were drawn tight against the night.

He shivered slightly and drew his dressing gown more closely round his shoulders. Soon now, he would have to face the moment that he'd dreaded. He would have to let Tim know about the next move that he'd planned. Not yet, though. That could wait a little longer. He brought his eyes back from the window, and thrust it from his mind.

Tim's voice had grown tenser.

"Come on, Jamie, we've got to admit it sooner or later, haven't we? If they're all accounted for, it looks as if it can only mean one thing, doesn't it? It can only mean—"

"*No.*" Jamie swung round now, to face him. "It can only mean somebody's lying, that's all. It's *got* to. Somebody's come out with something that isn't true, and we've been suckers enough to swallow it. OK?"

"And how are you reckoning on proving that, for God's sake? We might just as well jack it in right now and —"

"Look, just shut it a minute, can't you? And before we start jacking things in, you can give this the once-over." He fumbled in the pocket of his dressing gown and tossed a folded sheet of paper across the bed to Tim.

"What is it?"

"Well, look at it. You can read, can't you? Here's the torch. I want to know if I've made any gaffes, or left anything out. So just check it, OK?"

Tim fell silent and began to read the paper that he'd spread beneath his fingers. Above him, gigantic in the torchlight, his shadow-head moved darkly on the ceiling of the room. Jamie watched it, waiting.

Tim looked up now. He sounded slightly calmer than before.

"That's great, Jamie. It really is."

"Thanks. But I'm not asking for medals or anything. I told you—I just want to know if I've got it right."

"I'm dead sure you have. I'd say it's spot on."

"Yes. That's what I was afraid of."

"What d'you mean."

"What I said. Somebody's been lying."

"So . . . so you reckon there *is* something wrong on here after all?"

"I'm not sure. All I'm sure about is that the answer's on there somewhere. If we could only see it. It's *got* to be."

Tim's eyes turned back towards the torchlight on the paper. "The trouble is, when you see it all written down like this it seems to make it even more dead certain that the whole Committee was at home at eight o'clock." His silence came again. Then he slowly raised his head. "Jamie . . . what if he wasn't killed at eight at all?"

Jamie glanced up, frowning. "What?"

"Well, what if he died *before* eight? I mean, I know Doc Poole reckoned he'd been dead about an hour, but he couldn't be sure to the *minute*, could he? He said that himself to Grandad, remember? So what if it was ten to eight? Or

ONLY PEOPLE (apart from the 5 of us and O.J.) WHO KNEW WHERE THE KEYS WERE KEPT

	MOTIVE	PROBABLE MOVEMENTS 8:00 onwards	ALIBI GIVEN BY	OTHER INFO/QUERIES	WHAT THEY RECKON KILLED O.J.
POOLE	? (but see info column)	→ 8:10 at home 8:10-8:35 at Mrs. Brewster	Mrs. Poole Mrs. Brewer/ Mrs. Hammond	1. Inherited £120,000 from O.J.'s sister-in-law. 2. Accused by O.J. of being incompetent and responsible for her death (not proved). 3. O.J changed doors after her death.	Accident
OLD WILKIE	? (but see info column)	→ 8:50 at home	Joe	1. Reckons O.J. "got what was coming to him"(??) 2. Treated "like muck" by O.J. 3. Sacked from gardening up at H.H. by O.J. — 4. J accused by O.J. of thieving (not proved) / Reckons he'd 5. Believes in legend(??) possessed (??)	? (but something connected with the Power in the crypt)
GREGSON	£10,000	8:10 at home	Mrs. Hammond (spoke on phone)	1. Last person to see O.J. (5:45) ? 2. Guessed what happened in crypt. 3. Husband disappeared ages ago (??)	The Power in the crypt.

twenty to, even? That'd make a hell of a lot of difference, wouldn't it?"

"Yes. Except for one little thing you seem to've forgotten."

"What?"

"Well, if that's what happened, who rang the bell?"

"Oh." Tim looked away, and huddled even deeper in his blanket. "It always comes back to that in the end somehow, doesn't it? And it's that that makes the least sense of all, really."

"How d'you mean?"

"Well—*why*? I mean, why should anybody've wanted to ring the thing at all? You'd have thought that was the last thing they'd have wanted, sort of advertising it like that. And if . . . well, if somebody *did* do him in, why did they go and do it there? It's like Alex said—why couldn't they just've done it in the High House? D'you still reckon it was some kind of blind or cover-up or something?"

"Yes. At least . . . well, partly anyway. But there might've been an extra reason too, mightn't there?"

"An extra reason?"

"It was something your grandad said—you know, Monday afternoon, when he went through it in the dining room, remember? He said: *because* it happened up there, people were scared half out of their minds. Too dead scared even to talk about it in case something might—"

"OK, I remember. But I still don't get—"

"Well, knowing what Lychwood people are like, I can't think of a much smarter way of stopping them blabbing out info, can you?"

"Blabbing out info?"

"Yes. To the police."

"Hey . . . " For an instant Tim looked startled and excited.

Then slowly his excitement drained away. "But even if you're right . . . well, it still doesn't get us—"

"OK, you don't have to spell it out. It still doesn't get us any further with the eight o'clock alibis. There's still got to be somebody lying."

Tim chewed his nail in silence, his eyes fixed on the paper in his lap. "Look . . . what about Mrs. Poole?"

"Mrs. Poole? What about her?"

"She'd have a pretty good reason for lying, wouldn't she—saying the Doc was at home at eight o'clock when he wasn't? After all, they're husband and wife, aren't they? I mean, let's face it. If she knew what he'd really been up to, or even if she'd only put two and two together and *guessed* what he must've been doing . . . Hey, what's up, Jamie?"

"Sorry?"

"Are you listening?"

"Yes . . . yes, course I am." He reached across and took the sheet of paper from Tim's fingers. He gazed down at the writing, deep in thought.

Tim watched him for a moment, then sighed and shrugged his shoulders. "Anyhow, there's not a hope in hell we're going to be able to prove it, is there, even if she *is* lying? And even if we could, we'd still be no nearer figuring out the weirdest bit of all, would we? I mean, it's not only knowing *who* did it, is it? It's knowing *how*. It just seems impossible anyone *could've* done it, somehow."

Jamie raised his head abruptly, as if Tim's words had jerked him suddenly awake. The moment that he'd dreaded had arrived now. He knew he had to speak.

"Tim . . . just sit tight, OK, and don't start yelling me down or anything, but . . . Look, I know there doesn't seem much hope yet of saying for sure who it was who did it, but whichever of them it was, I reckon I . . ."

"You reckon what?"

Jamie drew a breath. "Well, I reckon I know how they might've worked it."

Tim was speechless. He stared at him, not moving, his face grotesquely frozen in the torchlight from below. "You know . . ."

"Yes. Or at least I . . . I think so. No, I'm *sure* I do. I've got to be right, Tim. There *could* only have been one way. And it all hangs on just three things. If I can only prove those, there's no way I can be wrong. I know there isn't."

Tim's words were voiceless. "Tell me."

And Jamie told him.

Then silence came again.

"So . . . so what d'you reckon, Tim? . . . It's got to have been that way, hasn't it? . . . If those three things are right . . . just a six-inch hole in the wall somewhere, *anywhere*, that's all it'd have needed. And if the stone's really not as heavy as it looked, and if we can prove it moves enough to—"

Tim's whisper cut him short.

"Prove it? How are we supposed to do that?" Jamie didn't speak his answer. His silence spoke it for him. And the answer turned Tim's face as white as death. "You don't . . ."

"Listen, Tim—"

"Jamie, you're not reckoning on . . ." As if an unseen hand had touched him, Tim's body flinched away.

"Look, it's the only chance of—"

"You're joking, aren't you?"

"No. Tim, listen—"

"God, you're crazy . . ."

"Hey, just listen, OK? Look, it's *got* to be like I said. And nothing's going to happen up there. The police were up there for months, weren't they, and nothing happened to them, did it? And we'd be together—there'd be the two of us, wouldn't there?"

"Like hell there would. You can count me out."

"Tim, it's our only chance—"

"No bloody way."

Jamie moved in closer. His voice grew taut and urgent. "Look, what if I'm right? What if it *was* done like that? OK, so I know it wouldn't prove which of them did it or anything, but at least it'd be *something*, wouldn't it? It'd prove there was a way of doing it, even in a locked room. And if we could just tell your grandad that much . . . well, maybe he could tell the village. Don't you see, Tim? At least they'd maybe start believing him that it wasn't . . ."

The words trailed away. This time, no answer came from Tim. He was shivering. The room had grown cold.

"It'll be OK, Tim. Just three things, that's all. And it'll be over."

"And what if we go in there and . . . and don't find what we're looking for?"

"We will, Tim. We've got to. It must've been done like that. There's no other way it could've happened."

Tim didn't turn to face him. His eyes looked out across the glimmer of the torchlight, gazing at the dark that lay beyond. Then his voice came, very quiet.

"Isn't there?" he said

15

---◆---

The Hammonds were departing. Car doors slammed on the far side of the cottage. The voices ceased abruptly and the silence came again.

Standing in the driveway against the pillar of the gateway, Tim and Jamie waited. They listened for the sound that would make departure real. For a moment there was nothing. Then the noise of the ignition shook the afternoon awake.

The car came into sight now. It jolted down the driveway and paused as it drew level. From the open nearside window Mrs. Hammond's face leaned out.

"We're on our way, then. Now you're sure you're going to be all right on your own for a bit?"

"Course we are, Gran. You just go and enjoy yourselves, OK?"

"Well, I don't know about that. The one blessing is that the weather's held off for us. I only hope it lasts, that's all."

Jamie followed her eyes upward. The snow hadn't come overnight. But its threat had closed in under cover of darkness. He could feel it above him, inching its way to the land.

"Still, we'll be fine, I'm sure, and it's only a few hours. You know where all the food is, so there's no need to go hungry. There's plenty of cold beef left, and you can manage to warm up some soup if you want it, can't you?"

"No hassle."

"If there's any problem about anything, you can always give Mrs. Gregson a ring. She does a bit of baking up at the High House on Sundays but she's usually home by about five. And don't forget I'll be phoning you myself before Evensong, at about five thirty."

"There's no need, honestly."

The vicar leaned towards them from the driver's seat beside her, and spoke across her shoulder with a wink. "What do you mean, no need? We thought it'd put your minds at rest, knowing the two old wrinklies have made it all the way to Blakeney with no bones broken."

"Point taken." Tim tried to smile. "Half past five on the dot then, Gran. We'll be here, ready and waiting."

Mrs. Hammond looked relieved. "Well, that's settled. You go on inside now. You're catching your deaths out here by the look of you, with no coats on."

"We're OK for a sec. We'll just watch you up to the end of the lane, then we'll get back in the warm."

"You do that. You're not thinking of going out again this afternoon, are you?"

"What?"

"This afternoon. You're not going out again?" A shadow of misgiving touched her eyes now. Her fingers tightened slightly on the glass. "Please don't, Tim. It's too cold. You will promise to stay in the cottage, won't you?"

Her words hung in the air between them. She waited for his answer. Jamie held his breath. Everything, he knew, was about to be decided. He knew what Tim was thinking: he couldn't break a promise that he'd made to Mrs. Hammond. And the promise would release him from the final crazy venture. It offered him his last chance of escape.

Tim spoke, and it was over.

"Don't worry, Gran. Even if we do, it won't be far. Five thirty on the dot, OK?"

The vicar revved up sharply. The time for talk had ended.

"Come on, Joyce, it's ten to three already. They'll be all right."

"Bye-bye then, both of you, and God bless . . . "

The window slithered upward, dividing her voice from them. The car moved quickly out into the lane.

They watched it growing smaller and pausing at the high street in a plume of gray exhaust fumes. It swung away and left them. They watched the grayness melting into air.

The west door grated open into darkness. They waited for a moment. Then they quickly slipped inside.

Tim closed the door behind them.

They looked up. They were standing in the tower. They couldn't see it clearly but they heard it, vast above them, in the emptiness of echoes. Only one thin line showed faintly, where the rope that hung beside them threaded upward into gloom.

They watched. No breath of movement touched it. They edged their way beyond it, to the nave.

They paused beneath the archway.

They'd paused here once before. Jamie looked around him, seeing it again. Strangely different. He'd remembered it by torchlight. But the light that he saw now came from the windows, and the day had almost faded. Dusk-light.

Less clear than he remembered, and less real. The silence was the same, though; and the smells. Smells of absence, of decaying. The death of wood and stone. There was nothing left here now except . . . He gazed out at the pillars, and followed them again into the darkness of the beams. This time, the darkness was unmoving. It wouldn't wake yet. It was sleeping. It was waiting for the coming of the night.

Tim shivered. His voice was only whispers.

"It's going to be pitch black soon, Jamie."

"It won't. Not yet. It's only ten to four."

"It's the snow. It's going to come, as sure as hell."

"We've got a torch."

Tim made no answer. He looked up at the windows. Then he turned his head and glanced back at the tower.

"What's up, Tim?"

"Nothing. Just making sure I shut the outside door, that's all."

"You . . . you left it unlocked, didn't you?"

"Yes . . . D'you reckon we were spotted?"

"From the High House?"

"No. I mean . . . well, from the village. Like last Tuesday."

"How should I know?" Jamie clenched his teeth to stop their rattle. "What difference does it make anyway? Stuff him."

Tim hugged himself more tightly. "God, it's cold . . . Jamie, this is crazy. What're we *doing* here?"

"You know what we're doing. We're looking."

"We *have* looked. And there's not a hole anywhere."

"We're not through yet."

"We've been over every inch of the crypt walls—"

"Only from outside. That means it's got to be in here, up there in the door-wall."

"Jamie—"

"Come on, let's get it over with."

"And what if—"

"It's *got* to be, OK?"

He moved, shying from Tim's answer, and set off up the nave, not looking back. The flagstones were encrusted with the debris from the rafters. His footsteps crunched soft echoes. He made his way alone. Then other footsteps came, which weren't just echoes. His breathing slowly steadied. Tim was following behind.

The crypt door lay in shadow. It was just as he'd first seen it, when the four of them had stood here. Only now a glint of steel showed replacement of the hinges; and the crowbar had left traces, in a line of pale scars.

Tim joined him. They both listened. No sound came from within.

"OK, then."

Jamie unshouldered his rucksack and dropped it beside him. The silence caught up the faint chink of the echo, metal on metal, pickaxe on shovel. He avoided Tim's eye.

"Let's get to work, Tim, shall we?"

"OK . . . what do we do?"

"Same as outside. We look."

They looked. They worked at the wall of the crypt from the nave side, probing it inch after inch with their fingers, pressing on every last crevice of stone. Nothing gave. Nothing yielded. The wall was intact, and sealed tight as a tomb.

Tim fell back, breathing hard.

"Let's pack it in, Jamie."

"Not yet."

"Look, it's no good starting on that bit again, we've covered it already. There's nothing here."

"There's got to be."

"Come on, just admit it, and let's get the hell out of here. You were wrong, OK?"

"Screw it."

"We've done all we can, Jamie—"

"Screw it, I said." He turned now, to face him. "OK, even if there isn't a hole, we can still prove the other things, can't we? We can prove the stone's not as heavy as it looks, and that it moves enough to —"

"What? They won't prove anything on their own—"

"Too bad. We can figure it out later."

"And . . . and what if we don't prove those either? When are you going to admit—"

"Look, I'm not going to believe it. Somebody did it. I'm not going to believe it was . . . Come on, let's get in here. You'll see, I promise."

"How long's it going to take?"

"What the hell difference does that make?"

"Gran's ringing at five thirty, isn't she, in case you'd forgotten?"

"So? We'll be home ages before that if we quit hanging round out here."

"But what if . . . what if the snow comes and they decide to turn round and head back? It'd kill Grandad if he found out we were—"

"He won't find out though, will he? He won't need to know anything unless we get the proof we're after. He'll reckon we've just gone for a walk like you told your gran."

Tim bit his lip. "I've left a note, Jamie. On the kitchen table. Saying where we've gone to. In case—"

"You've done *what*?"

"They'll find it when they get back."

Jamie's stomach tightened, as if the note in some way made the danger here more real. He fought the feeling down, and turned it into anger.

"Like hell they'll find it. By the time they get back, it'll be in the fire. It'll be in the fire by five thirty when your gran rings. And we'll be there to answer . . . So I'm going in, OK? If you want to come, that's great by me. If you don't, just sod off home."

"What's got into you?"

"Just hand over the key, right?"

"Jamie—"

"Are you scared or what?"

"Course I'm bloody scared!"

His voice rang loudly, up into the rafters and through the empty nave. Its violence shocked them both. Jamie stared at him in silence. Then he slowly dropped his gaze.

When he spoke, his voice was quiet.

"So am I, Tim. I can't do it on my own. Come with me. Please."

Tim closed his eyes. He didn't move. Then his shoulders answered for him. A tiny gesture, which might have been a shrug.

"It'll be OK, Tim, you'll see. As long as we stick together."

Tim's eyes opened now. A shadow of his old grin touched his face.

"OK," he said. "What the hell."

He reached into his pocket. His hand drew out the key.

The stone stirred, and rasped against the pickaxe. It rose above the narrow edge of earth.

A smell came from beneath it. The same smell which had

met them in the doorway. But stronger now, and colder. The smell of empty cellars. They felt its chill of dampness on their flesh.

"Hold it steady, Tim."

"I'm trying. It's too heavy."

"It can't be. It mustn't be. Just keep hold."

Tim's fingers whitened with the effort.

"We'll never shift it, Jamie. It's *massive*."

"The pickaxe is too small, that's all. It's only a hand-pick. The one last year was a hell of a sight bigger than this."

He rammed the pick in farther and heaved backwards on the handle. Iron bit more firmly on the underside of stone.

"For God's sake don't let go, Jamie. My fingers are underneath."

"I won't, I promise. Just hang on to it. I'm going further under."

He rocked the pick, and levered. The dead weight stirred again. The gap of darkness widened. Then Tim yelled. His hands released their grip as if the stone itself had burnt them. His face was white with horror. For an instant Jamie froze. The weight redoubled on the pickaxe. He felt the stone thrust downward. It strained against the handle. Then it held.

"God, Tim, what happened?"

Tim was on his feet now, his body flinching backwards, his eyes fixed with revulsion on the crevice where his hands had loosed their hold.

"Let it go, Jamie."

"What? What was it?"

"I don't know. Let *go*."

"Oh, come on—"

"There's something under there. I felt it."

"Pack it in, can't you? There's nothing there."

"It touched me."

"Tim—"

"It moved. It touched my fingers."

Jamie's blood ran colder.

"Come and grab this thing, Tim, I can't hold it much longer. Then I'll use the torch."

"It was soft."

"I'll have a look . . . Come *on*."

Tim came, and took the full force of the handle. Jamie crouched down with the torch. For a moment there was nothing. Then he saw the tiny movement. The earth beneath was squirming. The lifting of the stone had stirred the hidden night of insects. Their white and pulpy bodies wriggled downward from the light.

"What is it, Jamie?"

Jamie knelt back slowly. He felt his own flesh crawling now, as if they'd got inside.

"It's OK. It's only bugs."

"Bugs? What bugs?"

"Only slugs and things. They've gone now. Come on, let's get this filthy thing shifted."

They struggled on in silence. The hand-pick that they'd brought was soon useless. After ten or fifteen inches it had lost its grip entirely. With the metal shovel acting as a buttress, their hands and arms took over for the rest.

Half kneeling and half sprawling, they heaved against the narrow end until they felt it rising. Then they braced it on their shoulders and their palms. Jamie paused, and fought for breath.

"Again, Jamie . . . Come on, it's crushing my shoulder off."

"Hang on, I'm trying to shift my hold."

"The next bit'll be the worst. It'll take its own weight after that."

"OK. Ready."

They heaved again. The stone gaped wider. Their knees slithered down across the edge that had once held it and groped to find some purchase.

"It's going. Shift over to the corner and get one hand on the long side. We've got to try and stand up."

They scrambled blindly to find footholds. Their bodies were half-crouched now, not kneeling and not standing. The stone was right above them. Its mass thrust down against them like a lid.

"Quick! *Now!*"

For a second it resisted. Then the whole slab levered upward. The loss of weight was startling. It was moving now without them. They stumbled in its shadow, scuffing gashes in the newly opened earth.

"Hold the bloody thing! It's going over!"

They held it, dragging it back upright as it quickened for the plunge. It wavered for an instant, then was still.

They stood there, breathing hard. Then the noise of breath subsided. The crypt was deeply silent. And the silence seemed to tell them for the first time what they'd done.

They looked together at the stone that stood between them. It was taller now than they were, its underbelly veined with the soil-tracks of the slugs. Then they gazed down at the rectangle of earth.

Jamie's whisper broke their stillness.

"OK, Tim?"

"Yes . . . Jamie—"

"Don't say it."

"It's true though, isn't it? There's not a chance in hell he could've shifted—"

"I don't know." But the spasms in his muscles told him what Tim said was right. "*We* did it, didn't we?"

"Oh come off it. There're two of us, aren't there?" Jamie didn't answer. He was frowning, staring down at nothing. "Jamie, what's up?"

"I'm not sure. It just struck me, that's all . . . Listen, Tim, maybe there *were* two of them."

"Two of them? Two of who?"

"Maybe whoever it was got the old man to help."

"What?"

"Maybe he was brought across here to help, then when the stone was shifted and everything was ready—"

"Pack it in, can't you?" Tim shuddered. "God, that's sick—Hey, what was that?"

They stiffened. Faintly, a sound had brushed the stillness. Their eyes went to the window, fifteen feet above them. The same sound came again.

Jamie drew a breath. "It's come," he said.

The old glass had been blind, and thickly leaded. But the new glass was transparent. They could see the touch of snowflakes on the blackness of the pane.

"Come on, Tim, it's nearly twenty-five past four. Let's finish it off. We might as well now."

"What?"

"Let's see it through."

"What good's it going to do, Jamie?"

"Search me. But the worst's over now."

"Is it?"

"Come on."

The stone set off on its final journey. They helped it,

rocking it gently from corner to corner. It walked in between them, making its way to the steps. The floor took its weight now. It gave them no trouble. It had followed the same route before.

At the foot of the steps they paused for a moment, bracing themselves for the effort to come. The snow was still falling. The window was clogged.

"We'd better have the torch over here now, Tim. It's OK, I've got hold of this thing, it won't topple."

Tim loosed his hold and left him. Jamie waited, looking at the steps. The torch swung round behind him. Beyond its beam, the shadows grew still darker. He turned his head as Tim came back towards him. His eye fell on the rectangle of soil.

The shovel and the pickaxe were no longer where he'd left them. Tim had moved them. They were joined now, handle upon handle at the center of the oblong. And their joining made a symbol of the cross.

He didn't meet Tim's eye.

"Ready, Tim?"

"Ready."

Tim laid the torch against the edges of two steps, tipped at an angle. Its beam fanned up the staircase like a spotlight, and ended in a circle on the door.

"Third step from the top's the one we're after. If we use the steps as a sort of lever, it should go OK. Right. Tip . . . And lift . . ."

The stone began to climb. Taking one tread at a time it heaved its ancient body upward, sawing out vast echoes.

"And slide . . . And tip . . ."

It slid. Then climbed and slid again, like the shuffling of old footsteps. Jamie felt his sweat run cold.

"One more . . ."

Its shadow reared up higher in the circle of the torchlight. It staggered for a moment. Then it stopped.

Their own shadows stopped beside it, bending double, struggling for breath.

"OK, Tim, we've done it . . . This last bit's got to be dead careful, or the bottom's going to slide off the step."

Tim's shadow looked up slowly. "D'you really thing we ought to?"

"Look, we haven't done all this slog for nothing, have we? It's proof we're after, isn't it? Come on, we've only got to tip it a couple of feet."

"What if it jams the door or something?"

"Save your breath." His hands eased gently forward. "Take the weight!"

The stone wavered, and quickened into movement. The upper edge tipped forward. It struck against its shadow on the door. They listened. Like a faint and muffled drumbeat, the echo boomed away along the nave. Then there was silence.

"That's it, Tim. It's held. Now we'll find out."

Even in the torchlight, Tim's face was deathly white. His answer was a whisper. "Go on, then."

Jamie faltered for a moment. Then he reached towards the latch. It lifted with a click from the iron tooth which held it. And he pulled.

"What's up, Jamie?"

The door had made no movement.

"It's OK." He pulled again. A shiver touched his backbone. "You haven't locked it, have you?"

"Course I haven't locked it. Get out of the way a minute." Tim edged him aside and wrenched at the door latch. His wrenching grew stronger. The door moved a hair's-breadth, then closed again under the stone. He looked round, staring wildly. "Well, don't just stand there. Do something, can't you?"

"Look, it's going to be OK—"

"*Do* something!"

Tim clutched at the stone. He fought to release it. The weight of its angle resisted. The buttress of granite held firm.

Jamie saw him fall back. He struggled to salvage his last shreds of calmness.

"Tim, hang on, OK? We'll try the latch again. The stone's going to move like I said, right? Enough for us to slip out—"

Tim swung round to face him. "Screw it! And screw your bloody proofs! *We're trapped!*"

His panic sparked panic in Jamie. "Get the pickaxe!"

"What?"

"The pickaxe! We'll lever it off!"

Tim froze, looking back at the place where he'd left it. His panic was turning to dread. "But—"

"Get it! *Quick!*"

Tim stumbled away down the staircase. The steps were still spotlit. But beyond them the darkness had gathered, seeping its way through the crypt. Jamie watched as Tim grabbed for the torch at the bottom. Its beam left the staircase and plunged him in blackness, swiveling round to the oblong of earth. The cross of the handles leapt suddenly clear now. Tim hurried towards them. His fingers reached forward. The sign of the cross sprang apart.

And then the bell rang.

A single stroke, dying away into silence. The sound of it turned them to stone.

Then the silence was broken. Jamie was only aware of his

screaming and wrenching. The pain in his shoulders. The stone inching backwards. His body, and Tim's, squeezing out through the narrowing crack. His feet in the nave, and Tim's footsteps behind him. The arch to the tower. The bell rope still swinging. The door dragging open. A blizzard of light.

In the swirl of the snowflakes a shape loomed up blackly. White hands reached towards him. The fingers took hold.

16

It was five to five.

They sat by the stove in the kitchen of the High House. Their shivering had stopped now. The tea had helped to warm them.

They looked across.

Mrs. Gregson was in profile, unmoving, propped against the sink. The blackness of her dress was stained still blacker where the snow on it had melted. The rolling pin was lying where she'd dropped it when the tower bell had rung. She'd been baking when she'd heard it. She'd wiped the flour from her hands now but her wrists still bore its traces, and smudges of it clung to their own shoulders where she'd gripped them as they'd raced out of the church. She'd hardly spoken since she'd caught them. And she didn't look towards them even now. Her face gave no clue to her feelings. Perhaps its whiteness came from pity, and concern for what they'd been through. Or perhaps it came from anger, or from shock.

The same confusion of emotions showed in Alex. The same question he'd just asked was asked again.

"What made you do it?"

They glanced at him, but neither of them answered.

He was standing by the table, leaning forward, his knuckles bunching pleats across the cloth. His hair was wet, and clogged with sawdust. The ringing must have reached him in the woodshed on the far side of the courtyard. By the time he'd dashed towards them through the snowstorm, Mrs. Gregson had already taken hold.

"Well?"

Their eyes avoided his and dropped back to the teacups. There was no way of explaining, of making him believe them. The whole thing now seemed crazy, unreal beyond belief.

"You owe us *some* explanation, don't you? What were you doing in there? Oh come on, can't you? What made you do it? Why did you ring it?"

The silence lengthened. Tim's answer scarcely broke it.

"Alex, we didn't."

"I asked you *why*, not *whether*."

"We didn't. We swear it."

"We all just imagined it, then, did we?"

Tim closed his eyes. "I don't know."

"For God's sake, Tim—"

"We didn't ring it . . ."

His voice choked, full of tears. For a moment Alex watched him. Then something deep inside him seemed to crumble. His anger drained away now. Only weariness and pity still remained.

"OK." He fumbled for a chair and slumped down limply. "Let's leave it. We'll talk about it some other time, shall we?"

"Yes."

They lapsed back into silence. No one moved. Jamie listened to the pattering behind him, the fingers of the snow against the glass. Then the sound was strangely distant, and changed into the crackle of the wood stove. The heat was growing heavy, like sleep inside his eyelids. He let it come.

Then voices in the darkness. Tim and Alex speaking. Somewhere close beside him, yet very far away.

"Why don't you and Jamie go and get cleaned up a bit? You can have a bath if you want one."

"A bath?"

"Have you seen what you look like?"

"Oh . . . no, I hadn't really thought."

"And you want to get some iodine or something on those hands. If your gran saw the state of you, she'd have a fit."

"Oh God . . . What's the time, Alex?"

"Nearly five past—why, what's up?"

"We've got to go."

"Nonsense, you're going to stay here and have some supper. Then I'll—"

"We can't."

"What?"

"We can't. Gran's ringing the cottage at half-past. We've got to be there. We promised."

The voices ebbed, then surged again more loudly, like voices in a seashell. And Jamie sensed that Tim had left the wood stove and was calling him from somewhere near the door.

"Jamie, come on, we've got to go . . . Thanks for the offer, Alex, but there's no need, honestly, not in this snow. We'll be OK."

"Well, if you're sure . . . You'd better take a torch, in case. You can let me have it back some other time . . ."

Then blackness for an instant. The words inside the seashell swooped and faded.

". . . Mrs. Gregson's going to look in on her way home, just to see you're all right."

"Yes . . . Jamie, come on . . ."

". . . I've got a bag of kindling wood for your grandad. It's not very heavy. I'll bring it round from the yard . . ."

". . . Jamie . . ."

". . . If you go out the front way, I'll meet you on the steps . . ."

". . . Jamie!"

Jamie started, jolting half awake. A hand had touched his shoulder.

"Get a move on. We're off."

"Oh . . . Right."

He struggled to his feet. The heaviness of sleep had filled his limbs now, filled the kitchen. He waded through it, over to the door. He dimly knew that Alex wasn't with them. But somewhere in the distance Mrs. Gregson was still standing. He left her there, and hurried after Tim.

The passageway was dark, and unfamiliar. Tim had stopped halfway along it, at a door.

"I'm just going in here, Jamie."

"What?"

"In here. To the john. D'you want it as well?"

"No."

"I'll see you at the front door in ten secs then, OK? Alex is bringing the firewood round from the back."

"The front door?"

"You know the way, don't you?"

"I . . . I'm not sure."

"Just turn left at the end of the passage, and the first right'll bring you out into the hallway. That's where we came in last year, remember? See you there."

Tim vanished. The door clicked shut behind him.

Jamie willed himself back into motion, on along the passage. Then he turned the final corner and stopped dead. Tim was right. The corridor had brought him out into the hallway. He remembered. He was back again, back where he had started. This was where he had come in.

Last year . . .

He looked up at the ceiling, half expecting sounds of footsteps in the corridor above him. Tim's footsteps, when he'd run to fetch the blankets. While he himself had gone to find . . .

He remained where he was for an instant, staring numbly around him. Then he forced his feet forward.

He stood at the door, and looked in.

There was a fire in here, sputtering with logs. But the place looked cold. Too long for a sitting room; too dead. There was only one lamp, on a desk at the farthermost end. Two pools of lamplight, on ceiling and desktop . . .

He made his way over. Then stopped. He had almost trodden on something that must have blown from the desk. A sheet of paper, half written. He laid it on the desktop and anchored it in place . . . The pool of light spilt across it. He paused and looked down . . .

He didn't hear the footsteps behind him. Tim's voice came, like a blow in the stomach. He started with shock.

"Are you ready, Jamie?"

"What?"

"I said, are you ready? Anything wrong? What've you found?"

And, at last, Jamie knew what he'd found. He remembered what was wrong there. And the memory woke others, as if a single chain linked them.

The words of Mr. Hammond, in the dining room on Monday:

That was one of the things that puzzled the police. How he'd done it, I mean. Apart from the few obvious bits and pieces he had in his pockets . . . he hadn't brought anything with him except the stuff we saw on the floor.

And his words to Dr. Poole by the body in the crypt:

I haven't seen the lamp and pickaxe before, but the shovel's certainly his. It's one of a pair from his sitting-room grate . . .

Jamie looked across at the grate. Yes, back in place now. Hanging symmetrical. Heavy black iron.

The chain of the memories slowly assembled. And soon he would know where the chain was leading. He followed it, blindly, link by link. The paper. The words of the vicar. The black iron shovel. And the grate . . . The last time he'd looked at the grate was when—

There was a sudden crash behind them. They leapt together and swung round.

"God, what a fright. It's one of the logs, that's all. How the hell do we get it back in the fire?"

And, suddenly, he knew.

He didn't hear the footsteps behind him. Tim's voice came, like a blow in the stomach. He started with shock.

"Are you ready, Jamie?"

"What?"

"I said, are you ready? Anything wrong?" Tim's voice faltered. "God, what's up? Are you feeling OK?"

"I . . . I don't know . . . Yes, I'm OK."

"You don't look it. Don't keel over now, *please*."

"No . . . Just let's get outside, Tim. I want some fresh air, that's all."

The air came, in an icy blast of snowflakes as they opened the front door. A wind was rising strongly. Alex struggled through it round the corner of the High House, and handed them the torch and bag of firewood. They said goodbye and left him.

Tim set off fast along the pathway leading down towards the cottage. Jamie followed him in silence. He walked like someone sleeping. It was when they reached the beech trees that he stopped.

"Can I have the torch, Tim?"

"What?"

"The torch. Can I have it?"

"You can if you like."

"Thanks."

"I shouldn't think it'll be much use in this snow, though. As long as we just stick to the path, we'll—hey, where are you off to?"

"Just wait there. Don't move, OK?"

"What the hell—"

"I won't be more than a minute, I promise."

"Jamie!"

"Don't move!"

He ran, stumbling through the snowdrifts. The church rose up to meet him. The west door was still open. He quickly went inside.

He switched on the torch. The beam flew out into the darkness. It hovered for an instant, then it settled on the bell rope. The place where hands would hold it. Then it left it. It had found what it had wanted. It clicked back into darkness, and was gone.

Tim was still beside the beech trees. He didn't speak when Jamie came to join him. He turned away, tight-faced, and made for home. Jamie followed, but he didn't break their silence. They reached the cottage just on half past five.

The first words Jamie spoke came in the gateway, as Tim raced up the path to the front door.

"I . . . I'm not coming in just yet, Tim."

Tim halted in his tracks and swiveled round.

"*What* did you say?"

"I'm not coming in yet. I've got to see somebody."

"*See* somebody?"

"I've got to, Tim."

"What are you on about?"

"I'll be back soon. It's not far."

"How far? Where the hell are you going?"

"To Old Wilkie's."

Tim froze, staring at him blankly through the flurries of the snow. He didn't answer.

"I'll see you, Tim, OK?"

Jamie turned to leave him. For an instant Tim stood rigid. Then he moved. Jamie felt the impact as the hand closed on his shoulder. The fingers tightened, bunching up his flesh. And suddenly a sound shrilled through the silence. In the cottage, the phone began to ring.

For another moment Tim remained there, helpless. Then his words choked out, half anger and half tears.

"You're bloody cracked, you know that?"

His fist unclenched and jolted Jamie backwards. He rushed into the house and slammed the door.

Old Wilkie stood at the window. He seemed to be staring out. But there was nothing left to see there. The window-panes were white.

Close behind him, Jamie stood unmoving. Not frightened; only tired. He would like to go to sleep now. It was warm in here, and quiet.

Nothing had been spoken. It had been the same as last time. The old man had been waiting, and knew why he had come. He had come to ask a question.

He asked it now, simply and directly.

For a long, long time, it seemed, Old Wilkie didn't answer. Then he spoke one single word. It was enough.

Jamie's hand reached out across the silence. He touched the old man gently.

"It'll be all right, Mr. Wilkie, you'll see."

For the only time, the face came round towards him. Then Jamie turned, and left.

He paused just once before he reached the roadway. He looked back at the window of the room. The panes were thick with whiteness, but the face, he knew, was still there as he'd left it. Staring blindly outward, through the snow and through the tears.

Tim was in an armchair, right against the hearth. He heard the front door open; the footsteps in the hallway; and Jamie close behind him. He didn't turn to face him.

"Tim . . ."

"Gran sends her love."

"Tim—"

"And Mrs. Gregson called in, to check we were OK. I told her we were just great. She was really glad to know you were back to your old cheerful self and having a nice hot bath."

"I've got to talk to you."

"That'll make a change. I'm flattered. Go right ahead."

The silence was too long. In spite of himself, Tim looked round. Then he leapt to his feet.

"Bloody hell, Jamie, what is it? Hey, come on, sit down. Get right up to the fire . . . God, you look awful."

"We've got to get somebody here, Tim."

"What?" Tim glanced suddenly round to the window. He seemed to go cold. "What happened down there?"

"It's not that. It's . . ."

"OK, don't try and talk for a sec. Look, you just sit there and I'll get some coffee or something—"

"We've got to phone somebody."

"Jamie—"

"We've got to *tell* somebody. I'm scared."

"Tell them? Tell them what?"

"I know what happened, Tim. I know who did it."

17

---◆---

Alex had arrived.

He sat facing them across the kitchen table. For nearly fifteen seconds he didn't make an answer to Jamie's first announcement. And even when he spoke his tone was still uncertain, as if he doubted that he'd heard right or feared he was the victim of a hoax.

"Say that again, Jamie."

"We had to talk to someone, Alex. We know what happened to your uncle. We know who did it."

Jamie heard his own voice speaking as if it wasn't his at all but someone else's, someone very distant. Its calmness was unreal. Everything about him was unreal now. His weariness had left him. Or perhaps he'd passed beyond it. His brain felt clear as crystal, and sharply wide-awake.

"Jamie, are you serious?"

"Yes."

Alex hesitated, speechless. He slowly looked at each of them in turn. The sight of Tim seemed somehow to convince him. Tim's face was numb and rigid, and the eyes were out of focus, as if he was half-sleeping.

"OK, I can see it's no leg-pull. It'd be a bit too sick if it was. But . . . well, you must admit, it's rather hard to swallow."

"Sorry, Alex." Tim's voice came, but only with an effort. "We knew it was going to upset you. But we *had* to tell you."

"That's all right." Alex drew a breath. "Look, let's take things one step at a time, shall we? I can see how serious you are, but . . . I mean, there's a fantastic difference between *thinking* you know something, and knowing it for sure, isn't there? So—"

"We know for sure," Jamie said.

Alex paused, then slowly tried again. "OK. I accept that. So the first thing is: *how* can you be sure?"

"We've been working on it. We wanted to help. We've been visiting people and digging out info. And . . . well . . ."

"And doing a bit of sightseeing in old churches?"

"Yes."

"That fits."

"Alex, please listen. You've got to believe us . . ."

"I do believe you. I believe you mean every word you say. But that's not enough on its own, Jamie, surely you can see that? This is too serious to—"

"I know it is. That's why we phoned you. You've got to listen. It's not just guesswork, we've got all the facts worked out. We'll go through them from the beginning and if there's anything, *anything*, you reckon we've got wrong, you've only got to come out with it and we promise we'll admit we've made a cock-up of it and that'll be the end of it."

"Fair enough."

"But we're not wrong, Alex. You'll see. There was only one way it could've happened. And only one person who could've done it—"

"Fine. I said I'm ready to listen. From the beginning, though. And if you want to give me a chance of picking holes, you'd better take it slowly and don't both speak at once."

Tim looked up, heavy-lidded. "Don't worry about that, I don't reckon I could cope with it at the moment. Jamie'll do it best, anyway. He was the one who worked it out."

"OK, Jamie. Let's have it."

Jamie sat back slowly in his chair. His eyes grew distant, gazing beyond Alex, beyond the kitchen, out into last year. Behind where Alex sat the glass pane of the door showed only darkness, and snowflakes that were tapping to come in. Then suddenly he started. His eyes regained their focus. The darkness on the glass had shown a movement which wasn't just the movement of the snow.

Alex looked at him and swung round sharply. "What's up?"

He didn't answer. They listened. Then Alex left his chair. They watched him as he stepped across the kitchen. His hand paused for a moment on the door latch, then he wrenched it quickly open and looked out.

They held their breath.

Snowflakes gusted in across the tiles. Alex closed the door and then came back.

"It's all right. There's nothing there. This thing's just making us a bit edgy, that's all. Come one, let's get it over with."

Jamie's breathing grew more steady. He looked across at

Alex and felt glad that he and Tim weren't here alone. Then he heard his own voice speak.

"It's hard, really, to tell it in order, because it's all been such a muddle, lots of different bits that didn't fit. I suppose the answer was there all along, staring right at us if only we could've seen it. But it wasn't till today that the last bit came and hit me and that sort of locked all the other bits together . . ."

He paused, knowing that he'd come too far already. His thoughts went back, to where it all began.

"When we started out, talking about it in London and the first day up here, we had to reckon on four ways it might've happened. There was suicide, or accident, or murder. Or it could've been . . . something else, something from under the stone. Well, it was pretty obvious it wasn't suicide. And the accident idea seemed crazy, somehow. The police didn't go for it, for a start. There were Tim's gran and grandad, of course—they told us over and over how much they believed it. Especially Mr. Hammond. But I somehow got the feeling that even he wasn't quite so sure really, not deep down. Perhaps it was what he *wanted* to believe, that's all . . . Well, anyway, that left us with just two other ways. And we had to go for the murder idea first—then if that turned out to be a non-starter, we'd know . . . we'd know the villagers were probably right. So we knew we'd got to forget about the legend and everything. It wasn't very easy, really. It sort of kept coming back and muddling things up. Actually, we went up to the church on Tuesday as well as today—not inside or anything, but even from outside we got dead scared. I reckon it was after that that it really hit me what a brilliant place it was for a murder."

"I don't follow."

"Like I said, it muddled things up and got people thinking in the wrong direction and everything. Tim's gran said that too—about making connections where there weren't any. She said the legend had a weird power over people's minds. And it even made people too scared to talk about it for ages. So it must've been pretty tough for the police trying to get info, mustn't it?"

"Yes, I think it probably was. Go on."

"So we started on the detective stuff. The trouble was that we were up against two things instead of just one—it wasn't just finding out who'd done it, it was finding out how it was worked as well. By the look of it, it just couldn't have happened, because the thing we knew for sure was that the door really *was* locked, as well as having the stone against it, and there wasn't anybody else in there."

"But now you think there was? And yet we all looked through—"

"No. Apart from the body, the crypt was empty all right."

Alex frowned. "OK."

"So it really was brilliant—to use the crypt, I mean. And the stone being lifted sort of clinched it. What else *could* people reckon except that it must've been because of the legend? See what I mean?"

"Yes, I see that. But if the crypt was empty—"

"So the next thing was to try and figure out the motives and alibis. And that's where we really knew we were up against it. It was like Tim said: we dug up so much stuff we'd never even thought of, that there didn't seem a hope of finding out what was important and what wasn't." He stopped for a moment, and handed a folded sheet of paper across the table. "This is a sort of chart I did of it all. I showed it to Tim last night."

Alex took it from him and slowly read it through.

"How on earth did you get all this?"

"Oh, that was Tim. I suppose people don't clam up so much when it's somebody like us—not like they do with the police, I mean."

"And why these names?"

"Because it was only the Committee who knew where the church keys were kept in the dining room. So it seemed pretty obvious that one of them must've taken them and gone up some time after seven. Considering your uncle hadn't been dead for more than an hour, that ruled you out—"

"Thanks."

"And Tim's gran and grandad. So I was left with those names."

"Fine. And what did you make of all this info?"

"Well, I reckoned there were all sorts of motives there by the look of it, not just the obvious one of mon—" He stopped again, and bit his lip.

"You might as well go ahead and say it. The money motive." Alex smiled wryly. "I don't think the police missed it either, judging by the drilling they gave me."

"Yes. But there was Mrs. Gregson too, wasn't there? And even if other people's motives were a bit more muddled, we still had to reckon on the chance that the answer was there somewhere if we could only spot it. Old Wilkie really had it in for your uncle, especially after Joe and the thieving business, and them being sacked from the gardening job. Then there was the Poole hassle with the money your gran left them, and your uncle accusing him of things and changing his doc straight after. Then there was this missing husband of Mrs. Gregson's . . . Any of it might've been what we were after. Or it might all just've been leading nowhere. So, like I said, there didn't seem a cat's chance of figuring it out that way. I reckoned the best thing was to come at it from another angle and tackle the alibis. If they turned up trumps, the motive might fit in later with what we'd found."

"You've been methodical, I'll give you that."

"We had to. But the trouble was that the alibi angle didn't seem to work out either. Everyone who knew where the keys were kept was vouched for OK for about ten past eight, most of them by somebody really reliable like Tim's gran or Mrs. Brewer. But for eight o'clock the alibis were hopeless, because they all just said they were at home. It was pretty clear that somebody was lying, but we weren't exactly likely to be able to prove it. So that left us with another wash-out.

"That was when I knew there was only one hope left, just one more angle to work from. Not *who* did it, but *how* it was done. That might sort of click everything in place. And if that failed too . . . But it didn't. It turned up the answer.

"The more I thought about it, the clearer it got. It's like Tim said in the Bakehouse: if it *was* murder, the murderer had to get out somehow *and* lock the door. But there weren't any tunnels or anything, and nobody could've got through the window. That only left one other way out, didn't it? The door. So I made that a kind of starting point. And I reckoned it could've been done OK, so long as three things could be proved."

"The door? But the stone was—"

"Yes. So the stone had to be one of the three things. And it worked. If you wrench hard enough, the stone moves enough for you to be able to slip out and then drops back in place."

"Hang on . . . theoretically it might, but—"

"Oh, it's still there now, to prove it, against the inside of the door. We did it this afternoon."

"You did *what*?"

"We had to. It was panic, really. We thought we'd gone and got ourselves trapped in there. But it worked, anyway. And so that was that. First proof. The murderer could've just slipped out, then locked the door."

Alex drew a breath, as if struggling to grasp what he was hearing. "But the keys were *inside*, Jamie. They were by Uncle's body."

"That's where my second proof came in. There had to be a hole. If there was a hole somewhere, anywhere in the crypt walls—not a big one, just big enough for a hand to go through— it would've been easy, wouldn't it? Just chuck the keys back inside once the door was locked."

"And you looked for that this afternoon as well?"

"Yes. We covered every inch."

"And you found it?"

"No."

"You didn't? So in that case . . ."

"We must've missed it."

"Oh, come *on*—"

"The point is that I knew it'd *got* to be there. Not just to prove that bit of my theory, but because there wasn't any other way of explaining something else, something that really spooked me when I remembered."

"Something else?"

"Yes. You see, the keys had moved."

Alex stared at him. "*What* did you say?"

"The keys. They'd moved. It only hit me when I went back up to the church with Tim on Tuesday, than again when we were talking to Mrs. Poole. It all came back, just like I'd seen it that first time. When we looked through the window the keys had been just in front of your uncle's hand, as if he'd been trying to reach them, right?"

"Yes . . . yes, I think so."

"But when the door caved in, they weren't there any more. Not by his hand. They were by his shoulder."

Alex seemed to turn cold. "They can't have been."

"They were. They'd moved."

"God, Jamie, what are you getting at? Look, wait a minute. You must've seen wrong. If there wasn't a hole, they couldn't have moved on their own, for heaven's sake. The only other possibility is that whoever it was was still in there when we looked through the window. And we *know* there was nobody there but Uncle—"

"It wasn't your uncle in there, Alex. Not when we looked through the window."

"*What?*"

"It's the only logical answer, isn't it? It was somebody else who was pretending, somebody wrapped up in your uncle's overcoat and scarf. We couldn't see the head, could we? We didn't see that till we broke through from the other side. It wasn't your uncle. It was somebody who was still alive."

"You're crazy . . ."

"No. I can prove I'm not."

"*Prove* it?"

"Yes. I've proved it already. I visited there this afternoon. He told me."

"Visited? Visited who?"

"Old Wilkie."

"Old Wilkie?" Alex turned white with shock. "But . . .you're not suggesting an old man like that dragged that—"

"Oh no. It wasn't him. It was Joe."

Silence came, sudden and cold. It was Jamie himself who broke it.

"Who else could it've been, Alex? At eight fifteen when we looked through the window, the others seemed to be accounted for, by Mrs. Brewer or Tim's gran. And it couldn't have been *Mrs.* Poole, could it? She couldn't have shifted that stone. Like I said, somebody on that chart had to be lying. It was Tim who gave me the clue, last night in the bedroom. He said why shouldn't Mrs. Poole be lying to cover up for the Doc—they're husband and wife, after all. And it suddenly hit me that the same could be said about the Wilkies too—why shouldn't Joe lie to cover up for his dad? But, like you said, Old Wilkie couldn't have shifted that stone. So what if it was the other way round? What if Old Wilkie was lying to cover up for his son?"

"But—"

"Because he did know, Alex—he knew Joe had been there. When Joe got home, he must've looked as filthy as we were this afternoon. He wouldn't have let on to his dad, but Old Wilkie couldn't have been in the dark for long, not once your uncle's body was found. I reckon he guessed just what'd happened then. And I bet he's been through hell ever since. You see, he really believes in this crypt thing, like a sort of power or something that keeps coming back and getting in to people. When we went to see him the other day, he went on as if he reckoned he was possessed or something, sort of taken over by it. As if it'd made him kill your uncle. But I got that the wrong way round too. It wasn't him at all. He thinks it's got in to Joe."

"But you can't take that seriously, for heaven's sake. He's *senile*."

"Maybe. But he seemed to sort of know why I turned up there this afternoon, even so. As if he'd been waiting for it. Kind of knowing it was all over. I just asked him if Joe was *really* there that night, having supper in front of the telly. And he said no."

"Jamie, now *listen* . . ." Alex's face had tightened. "Why should Joe of all people—"

"Don't you see how brilliant it was? The one person nobody'd think twice about. The bloke who can walk into people's houses with boxes of groceries, like he walked in here on Monday—right past the dining-room door. With Tim's gran stuck inside the kitchen doing her washing like she does every Monday. *Every* Monday, Alex. The old Lychwood routine. Same things same time every day. But even then I didn't twig it. Because I was still stuck with the obvious idea of the Committee people in there from six till seven, just like the murderer *wanted* everybody to be stuck with it. I never even bothered to think that anybody on the Committee could've told somebody *else* where the keys were. Oh yes, Joe got those keys all right, on Monday afternoon. And all he had to do after the murder was to come back up to the crypt when the crash came as if he didn't know a thing. So even if he'd left any traces of himself around the place, they'd all be explained."

"Jamie, this is getting beyond *anything*, and you know it. It wouldn't be so bad if it made any sort of sense at all. But it doesn't. Even leaving aside the fact that there's not a reason on earth why Joe should've gone in for all this crazy fancy-dress nonsense in the crypt at all, who's supposed to have told him where the keys were kept? *He* wasn't on the Committee, was he? So the only person who could've told him was Old Wilkie. And yet you just said Old Wilkie hadn't got any idea of what was up until Joe got back after the—"

"But it wasn't Old Wilkie who told him, Alex."

"What? Are you seriously suggesting that Joe asked somebody *else* on the Committee where the keys were, and then hoped they'd forget all about it after he'd gone and murdered my uncle?"

"Murdered your uncle?" Jamie looked startled. "Oh no, it wasn't *that* I meant . . . That wasn't Joe. Joe wasn't the murderer."

"Wasn't . . ."

"Joe was just the stuntman. There had to be two people, you see, for it to work."

Alex didn't answer. He looked stunned.

Jamie hardly seemed to notice. "I never reckoned on that. I was banking on the stone being lighter than it looked, so it could be shifted by one person. That was the third proof I was after. It hit me I was on the wrong track up in the crypt today, when Tim pointed out it'd taken *two* of us to do it. But I still didn't quite twig. I thought whoever it was might've got your uncle to help. But that didn't make any sense. I mean, why should your uncle have helped anyone shift that thing against the door? No, Joe and the murderer did it together. And Old Wilkie still doesn't know that. The poor old bloke still reckons it was Joe who did for your uncle. No wonder he was trying to cover up."

For the first time, Alex's patience showed signs of giving way.

"And where's Uncle supposed to have been while all this

pointless rigmarole's going on, for God's sake? When's he supposed to have come across to the crypt?"

"He didn't come. He was brought. He wasn't killed in the crypt, you see. He was killed in his own sitting room."

"*What?*" Alex froze. "You're prepared to sit there and tell me that this murderer, or visitor, or whatever it is you're on about—"

"Oh, there wasn't any visitor. That wouldn't have made any sense either. It's like Tim said in the Bakehouse: nobody in their right mind would've taken a risk like that—what if your uncle had told you or Mrs. Gregson who was coming? I reckoned the person who planned all this had got a bit more up top than that. No, like I told you to start off with, it suddenly hit me this afternoon that it *must've* been done in the High House. And then everything sort of clicked into place. It was when I was in the hall waiting for Tim— I took a look in the sitting room again, like last year, and it all came back. It was me who picked the paper up off the floor, you see—the one your uncle was writing that night, for his book. I put it back on the desk, because I thought it must've blown off from there. But it couldn't have, could it? Not on a night like that. There wasn't any wind. And there weren't even any windows open. And, anyway, it wasn't exactly likely your uncle wouldn't have noticed it, was it? But what if he didn't notice it because he *couldn't* notice it anymore? What if his own hand dragged it off the desk when he was heaved out of his chair? After somebody had cracked him from behind?"

"This has gone far enough!"

"Listen, Alex. *Please.* I know that's not proof or anything, but there's something else. You see, something happened when me and Tim were there that night—a log fell out of the fire. We had one hell of a job getting it back in. We had to do it with the only things we could find—the hearth-brush and the poker. We'd have used a shovel if there'd been one, but there wasn't. *It wasn't there.*"

"But good God, lad, of course it wasn't there! We'd just seen the damned thing, hadn't we, over in—"

"Not that one. The other one."

"The—"

"The matching one. Like Mr. Hammond said to Doc Poole that night in the crypt: the shovel was one of a *pair.* Well, that's right, isn't it? They're both back there now, aren't they? I saw them today. Don't you get it, Alex? The other shovel had to be over in the crypt by Joe's body, set up for when we looked through the window!"

"*Stop* this! Have you even *thought* about what you're implying?"

"Yes, of course I have—"

"Don't you realize what it'd mean if all this crazy nonsense was right? The person you're accusing of murdering my uncle would have needed inside knowledge of the House. And I mean *inside* knowledge. At least enough inside knowledge and opportunity to lay hands on Uncle's overcoat, his scarf, the shovel, everything. And the means of getting back into the House after seven o'clock without Uncle knowing, while he was writing at his desk . . ."

"That's right! The murderer *had* to have keys to the House!"

There was silence. For a moment which seemed endless Alex sat quite rigid. And in that moment, on the blackened glass behind him, it might have been that something even blacker stirred again. But Jamie hardly saw it. He was too far gone to care.

Alex fought to gain control.

"OK. Even if we accept that—and I'd better tell you now that I *don't* accept it, not even for a minute—what farce does it leave us with? We've got Joe Wilkie lying in the crypt for some godforsaken reason, posing as Uncle, to fool people looking through the window which it's somehow presumed they're going to smash. We've got somebody else killing Uncle over in the High House, then carting the body across to the church. And then what? Joe gets up and unlocks the door and wrenches it open?"

"Yes."

"And the real body's carried in and laid down? Joe and our murderer leave, locking the door behind them?"

"Yes."

"And then I suppose they look round for the famous hole in the wall, to chuck the keys back through?"

"No. Only Joe does that."

"And what does he do when he finds there isn't one?"

"But there is."

"Oh come on, damn it, you said you both looked and—"

"But there *is*, isn't there, Alex! Just think! The most obvious one of all!"

"Where the hell—"

"*The window.*"

"The—"

"The window, Alex. It's been smashed, hasn't it? And so Joe can do his stuff with the keys. He misfires a bit, but it's good enough. The door's locked. The keys are inside. And the murderer's in the clear—"

"Oh for God's sake!" It was over. Alex thrust his chair back. "This is bloody ridiculous! I've given you a fair hearing, but I'm not going to sit here—"

"Alex, *listen*—"

"Do you honestly expect me to swallow this? You start off by implying that the murder wasn't committed at eight o'clock at all. That it was committed when we were actually on the spot—"

"*Yes.*"

"Then you concoct some crazy scheme . . . And how long do you think it would have taken to carry out this so-called brilliant plan of yours? When's it all supposed to have happened?"

"But there *was* time—"

"How long was that door not being watched? Tell me that."

"I'm trying to. You're deliberately—"

"We smash the window. We look in at what's supposed to be my uncle, then we dash straight back round to the door. And in that time, murder's been committed, doors unlocked, bodies changed over, doors locked again, keys thrown through windows, and the culprits gone. And how long have they had to do it in while the door's unguarded? Twenty seconds? Thirty?"

"But that's not right, is it? What about the rest of the time?"

"The rest of what damned time?"

"The ten minutes you're forgetting about."

"*Ten minutes*? You're trying to tell me that the door was unguarded for *ten minutes*?"

"No, it was guarded all right."

"Oh for God's sake—"

"For ten whole minutes it was guarded by the murderer, wasn't it?"

"*What?*"

"There was only one person who had enough time to do it. There's only one person who *could've* done it, isn't there, Alex? And that's you."

18

___◆___

They watched each other, absolutely silent. So silent that the snow against the glass was like a drumbeat. And Jamie felt nothing. No weariness; no pity; and no fear. Not even calmness now. Only numbness. He was a thousand miles away, watching himself watching. And nothing but his brain seemed left alive.

Alex spoke. His lips and throat were rigid.

"I think you'd better retract that."

"I can't, Alex."

And the watching came again. Jamie wondered if they'd sit like this forever. But it didn't matter. Nothing mattered now.

The voice again. The eyes that didn't flicker.

"Then prove it."

And his own voice. He listened to it speak.

"I can tell you what I think happened, Alex. That's all.

"I don't know when you first thought of doing it. It doesn't matter now. And maybe it wouldn't have gone any further than thinking about, if it hadn't been for hearing about the legend. Maybe that's when you reckoned it was really on. It seemed to be just sort of crying out to be used. Just one day's work and you could clean up the lot—the cash, the High House, everything. And all it needed was a stuntman.

"The trouble was who it was going to be. Some friend or other from outside Lychwood would've been a bit risky, probably. He could've been spotted hanging round the Grounds up by the church, and people might've started asking questions. But somebody from *inside* Lychwood . . . somebody who liked a bit of a gamble. Somebody who really had it in for your uncle, and who was pretty strong, and good at doing things with his hands. Somebody who could come and go where he wanted, who could get hold of the keys on Monday afternoon if you told him where they were kept, and who could drive up through the Grounds in his grocery van with no questions asked. Somebody who was the *last* person anybody'd link with you. And—maybe this is what really clinched it—somebody who was dead hard-up for cash . . . Joe Wilkie.

"It all must've started looking good now. And what made it look even better was the Lychwood routine. Same things, same time. First Monday every month. Tim's gran up at the church for a clean-round till lunch, to swear everything was OK when she left there, even the crypt. Pre-Committee session down here at the cottage with Tim's grandad at half past five, with Mrs. Gregson staying on up at the High House with your uncle alive. A good load of suspects in the dining room from six till seven. You staying on for supper. And your uncle working at his desk and never coming down for bridge till nine on the dot. And by then it'd all be over.

"So on Monday afternoon it gets going. While you're still at the office in Wells, Joe gets hold of the keys and heads up to the church. Maybe you've already left the crowbar and lamp and pickaxe ready, under the bushes or something, so he can make a start on the crypt. You leave the office at the normal time and park the car somewhere in the trees in the Grounds. Then you give Joe a hand setting everything up. The stone's shifted against the door, and works OK if it's on the third step from the top. You leave him there, stick the crowbar back under the bushes outside the church on the way out, then make for the car again and drive on up to the High House as usual. Except that it's a bit later than usual now. But you'll tell Mrs. Gregson the traffic was snarled up on the way back from Wells. That's what she told us, as well, when we went to see her.

"She told us about the regular High House routine too. So I suppose that's what happens next. You unlock the front door like you always do and shout to Mrs. Gregson you're home. Then you go up and shower and change, which I expect comes in useful after the job you've done in the crypt. Tea on your own with your uncle, and wait for him to get back to his desk. Quarter past five. Mrs. Gregson's still out at the back in the kitchen. She hears you call out you're off now to the pre-Committee session with Tim's grandad. But she doesn't see what you're taking with you. A shovel from the sitting-room grate. And your uncle's overcoat and scarf from the hall . . .

"They're handed in to Joe on the way down to the cottage. And Joe can wait on a bit, then lock up and head back for the village any time he likes, ready to come back later.

"So it's all set up.

"Now comes one of the really brilliant bits. The first thing you do when you come down to the cottage is to give Tim's grandad the news: your uncle's come out with it over tea— he's been told something weird about the legend, and he's banking on a meeting to clinch it before he heads down here at nine . . . Even Mrs. Gregson told us how surprised she was your uncle had let on to you about it, considering how tight he was with his info where you were concerned. But we all swallow it OK. And why shouldn't we, really? What'd be the point of you telling us something that isn't true? But it *isn't* true, of course. There isn't any new info at all. Your uncle hasn't mentioned a word about legends and meetings or anything. It's your story, not his. And it does the trick. The legend becomes Topic Number One from then on. Me and Tim are busting to hear all about it. And you make it easy for us—you persuade Tim's gran there'll be no harm in telling us. So it's ghost stories round the fire. And it's what we're all thinking and talking about when the big moment happens. When the bell rings.

"The bell. The most brilliant bit of all. The one bit that didn't seem to make any real sense. Like Tim said, if it *was* murder, why should any murderer want to go and tell every-body he'd done it? But that's obvious now. Just one ring of the bell and three things were clinched.

"Number One: it's the signal from Joe you've been wait-ing for, fixed for eight o'clock on the dot. The signal for the off. And who's going to hear it but us? It's not likely anybody in the village will, and even if they do it won't make much difference—it's the vicar who's in charge of the church, so he'll be the one to go up. And—much more important—your uncle won't hear it, of course. Because he's as good as stone-deaf. He can hardly even hear his own doorbell . . .

"Number Two: it really does seem to clinch the legend all right. The bell rings, and somebody's dead. Just like it always happened in the old days.

"And Number Three, the greatest idea of all, the one everything depends on: the bell rings and somebody's dead. So if the bell rings at eight on the dot, somebody's dead at eight on the dot. The time of the death's fixed spot-on. And why should anybody even stop to reckon that your uncle hasn't been murdered at eight at all? That he's still over in the High House working away at his book?

"It should go like clockwork now. Tim's grandad's bound to insist on going straight up there. Which gives you just what's needed. A witness. And then there's the first hitch. *We* want to come too . . . But that seems OK, even if it hasn't been part of the plan. Even better in a way. Three witnesses now instead of one, and the best witnesses anybody could ask for, really. Not only a vicar, but two kids as well.

"So off we all go. The weather's just right, with the ground good and hard, so there'll be no awkward footprints or anything to explain away later, when things start happening up by the church. The lamp's on in the crypt, to lead us straight there. The door's locked and there's no way we're going to get through it using just shoulders. So we make for the only place we can—the window. And when that's smashed in, you're home and dry.

"We see what we're supposed to. The shovel, the pickaxe, the stone gone from its place and up against the door. And your 'uncle' stretched out there in his overcoat and scarf, feet to the window. Joe's done a good job. Then back round to the door. Now's the time to get rid of the witnesses. You suggest what we need is a doc. But there's no phone in the High House, of course, so there's only one answer. Tim's grandad even comes out with it himself: he'll head back for the village. And then the second hitch. I suppose you hadn't had time to think things through when you'd agreed we could come up to the church as well. And now we're not going back with the vicar. We're staying with you.

"But that's going to work out OK too. Just get rid of us

by packing us off to the High House for brandy and blankets. And, again, it seems even better than planned: we'll be able to swear Mr. Jefford had locked up behind him, and we'll actually see that the sitting room's nice and normal, with no signs of funny-business. But *before* all that happens, there's something important you've got to see to . . .

"You handle it really well. You tell us you're going to cut round through the paddock to pick up a crowbar from the yard at the back of the House. The doors round there are bolted on the inside—Mrs. Gregson's done that herself—so a trip to the *back* of the House looks pretty innocent. Then, even more innocent, you ask if we want to come with you. But not *both* of us, only *one*. You suggest the other ought to stay by the door of the crypt in case your uncle shouts out or something. And it's bound to work. Neither of us is likely to leave the other one behind in that place on his own. So we stick together. Which leaves the way clear for the biggest moment of all.

"You go to the High House round the front way and let yourself in with your keys. Into the sitting room. Your uncle at his desk with his back to the door. The second shovel from the grate . . .

"And it's over.

"But time's tight. Tighter than it was meant to be. It was meant to be at least twenty minutes while Tim's grandad was away. It's too tight now to notice little things like a paper that's dragged off the desk. Back now, as fast as you can to the church. Prop Mr. Jefford somewhere, and the shovel—round the corner, maybe—where he won't be noticed by us in the dark when we leave for the High House. Pick up the crowbar from under the bushes, join us again by the crypt, hand us your keys, and send us packing.

"Just gone half past eight. The coast's clear. Signal to Joe.

He unlocks the door from inside and wrenches it open enough for you to bring in the body. Set up the show together, making sure you change over the shovels, then both of you out through the door and lock up behind you. Joe's bit's nearly over. All he's got to do now is to head back for the village, slipping the first shovel in the bushes outside for you to pick up later, and pitching the keys through the window on his way round. A pretty good shot, as near as makes no odds, and he's gone.

"Just gone twenty to nine. And you can start work with the crowbar, and wait for us both to come back. It's been done in ten minutes. The impossible murder's complete."

For the first time, Jamie heard himself pause. Alex was unmoving. The kitchen was deeply quiet.

"And for a year everything's great. Then *we* come back. And we start snooping around. It must've made you start wondering, when you found we'd been down at Mrs. Poole's, and maybe you even knew we'd been to the church on Tuesday. Perhaps that was the idea of the tea in the Bakehouse, to see how much we'd figured out. Or it could've been to throw us off the scent or something. I don't know. It seems like that now, anyway. You even suggested the legend could be true after all. And you gave us plenty of info to back up our Doc Poole theories too. It was the only time you seemed to unwind a bit, when you could see he was our number one suspect.

"But it didn't stop us. I expect the village hot line soon gave you the news that we'd been to Old Wilkie as well, and Mrs. Gregson. And this afternoon really finished it. I suppose you spotted us coming up to the church again, when you were over in the yard. And this time we went right inside. When we didn't come out, you came round to the window to see what we were up to—only a quick look, but it was enough. There was only one way left to scare us off. The bell. And it worked.

"It's weird though, really. Because it was you doing that, that sort of clinched everything. If you hadn't, I don't reckon we'd ever have proved the stone idea. But we were so scared and wrenched the door so hard that the thing really did move enough to let us out. Then when I looked in the sitting room at the High House, things suddenly started fitting together. Not everything straight away, but enough for me to guess it must've been done in the House and not in the crypt. Which meant whoever did it must've had keys to get in. And that only left two people. I can see now it couldn't have been Mrs. Gregson, what with Tim's gran speaking to her on the phone and everything, but I wasn't thinking very straight this afternoon. So on the way down to the cottage I went back inside the tower because I knew now that whoever it was was panicking enough to have rung that bell. I shone the torch on the rope, where the hands would've been. It'd have shown straight away if it *had* been Mrs. Gregson—we had the shoulders of our parkas to prove it, where she'd grabbed us as we'd come out of the church. Because her hands had been covered in flour . . .

"So that left only you.

"I know none of all this is *real* proof or anything, Alex. I suppose you could still say it's all just theory. Except that there's one other thing.

"Like I said, it's weird, somehow. If it hadn't been for you ringing that bell, we wouldn't have come back to the High House at all this afternoon. And then I don't reckon I'd ever have remembered the one thing that really seems to clinch it. It was what I saw on that paper . . ."

He paused again. His eyes gazed out, unblinking, as if on something far away.

"It's worred me ever since I got back to Lychwood. I kept seeing that paper I'd put back on the desk, with the light on it, and your uncle's writing. And I knew I'd seen something wrong there. But I couldn't sort of bring it back. I kept going through the bits I could remember—about architecture and the cottages down in the village. But it still didn't click. And it was only this afternoon it hit me. It wasn't what I'd been thinking it was. It wasn't what your uncle had written at all. It was something else on the paper that was wrong, something I'd actually put there myself, to anchor it down with . . . It was your uncle's keys.

"It must've struck me the second I saw them. You see, I'd been looking at keys like that only a couple of minutes before. I'd been training the torch on them for Tim to open the door to the High House—the keys you'd given us to get in with. And here was another lot almost the same. Your uncle's house keys. And it made no sense at all. Your uncle had gone out, locked the door behind him, and left his keys on his desk? But of course it wasn't him who left them there, I can see that now. It was you. Like I said, time was tighter than you'd planned. You didn't have much chance to think. So you forgot to put your uncle's keys in his pocket before you carried him back to the church. And that one little thing could've ruined everything.

"But you remembered in time. I think you remembered when we got back to the church with the blankets and stuff, and Tim held *your* keys out to you. You looked so sort of stunned when he did that, and you didn't answer for ages. But maybe, you thought, it could still be all right. You took your keys off him and put them in your pocket.

"Then Tim's grandad came back with Doc Poole and the crypt door was broken in. You let Doc Poole go in front, just like you'd planned, so he'd be first to the body. And then you had to go through with something that probably wasn't in the original plan at all. You had to go down and clutch at your uncle. And slip your own keys in his pocket.

"Luck seemed to be on your side, really. You'd already remembered you'd asked Tim to leave the front door on the latch—you even asked him again when we got back to the church, to make sure he hadn't forgotten. So everything seemed fine—even if you hadn't got your own keys to the House anymore, you could still get back in. And everything *was* fine, except for one little thing.

"It was such a little thing that you just had to hope nobody would notice. And they didn't. Maybe I wouldn't have noticed either, if it hadn't been for seeing your uncle's keys on the desk and then remembering something I'd heard . . . There were two keys on your ring that weren't on your uncle's. Tim had tried to use one of them, in his rush to get into the High House that night. I remembered saying to him that it wasn't a house key he was trying, it looked like another sort of key altogether. And then, this afternoon, I recalled what Tim's grandad had said when he'd told us all about what the police had found out: *apart from the few obvious bits and pieces Mr. Jefford had had in his pockets— handkerchief and penknife and house and car keys and stuff* . . . Car keys, Alex. The key ring in your uncle's pocket had got car keys on it . . .

"And I remembered what you'd said yourself, that night on the way up to the church: *You know Uncle's views on motoring. He prefers to use his legs.* And what Mrs. Gregson had told us: *Alex persuaded his uncle to let him drive him into Norwich a few times, but even that was a battle. Old Mr. Jefford didn't hold with cars* . . .

"Your uncle's house keys were on his desk, Alex. And he had car keys in his pocket. But he didn't even drive.

And then silence. No sound, not even snowflakes. Everything was coming to an end.

There was nothing now but Alex. A face that watched and waited. And eyes as still as glass.

Jamie wasn't sure how long the silence lasted. Then Alex spoke.

"If I *am* a murderer, you've been taking a bit of a risk, haven't you?"

Jamie didn't answer. The face was still unmoving. But somewhere deep inside it, he knew a smile had come.

"All Lychwood tucked up nice and tight. Mrs. and Mrs. Hammond not due back for half an hour at least. And such a lot of snow. They might be late. They might be too late."

Jamie's numbness didn't leave him. His fear still didn't come. The words held no surprises. He'd waited for them, almost longed to hear them. At least, he thought, they meant that it was over. At last he'd reached the end.

But he hadn't. Not the ending he'd expected.

The face before him altered. The eyes dropped slowly downward. And the smile which had been hidden reached the surface. Not threatening; but infinitely tired.

"It's OK," Alex said. "Please don't be scared of me. You're not, are you?"

Jamie looked on, helpless. His answer wouldn't come.

Perhaps Alex didn't notice. He only smiled again.

"It's odd, really," he said, "but I'm glad. I'm glad you know. It helps, somehow . . ." He paused, then went on almost shyly. "I'd like to tell you something before I go. Maybe you won't believe it, but I'll tell you all the same. I've regretted what I did to Uncle, ever since it happened.

But do you know what I've regretted even more? It's what I did this afternoon. Ringing that bell. Not in the way you're thinking. I don't mean because it gave me away. I mean what I felt like, when I did it. What I knew I was doing to you. I think that was the loneliest moment of my life. Funny, isn't it?"

For a moment more he sat there, his eyes still gazing downward. Then he rubbed the tiredness from them, and stood up.

"Well, that's that. Except . . . well, to say thanks. For phoning me first, I mean, and . . . and giving me a chance. Sounds a bit crazy, doesn't it? But . . . well, thanks. Anyway, I'd better be on my way now, I suppose, while I still can."

For the first time, Tim raised his face towards him, and something Alex saw there made him pause. He turned back now to Jamie, slightly puzzled and unsure.

"You *did* phone me first, didn't you? You haven't let anyone else know? You haven't told the . . ."

Jamie's voice came very softly.

"We phoned them two hours ago. They came straight away. They asked us if we'd ring you and . . . and talk to you. So that they could . . . I'm sorry, Alex."

The two doors opened, from the garden and the hallway. The detectives who'd been posted came inside.

Alex didn't look towards them. He only looked at Jamie. Not with anger; but with puzzlement and hurt.

And Jamie's numbness left him. Something seemed to burst inside him. He dropped his eyes from Alex's, and cried.

19

———◆———

"**D**id we do right, Tim?"

"I don't know."

They stood beside the church. Down below them, in the cottage, their bags were packed and ready. They were leaving very soon.

Jamie shielded his eyes against the dazzle of the sky across the whiteness. The snow was deeper now than ever. But there would be no more.

On the coast road a snowplow moved minutely, making gray on white.

"They're clearing it," Tim said. "Which means the way to the station'll probably be OK. Which means school."

"I think I've outgrown it."

"You'll grow back. By tomorrow, this won't have happened."

"It will for Alex."

The snowplow moved on eastward. They watched it without speaking. It disappeared from sight.

"What d'you reckon they'll do to him, Jamie?"

"I'm not sure..." Jamie didn't turn to face him.

"Tim . . . wasn't there any other way we could've done it?"

"We had to phone them."

"I don't mean that. I mean . . . making him admit it, when we knew they were out there . . ."

"He wouldn't have admitted it to them. Only to us."

"That's what made it so horrible."

"I know . . . But there were other things that were horrible too, weren't there? I don't mean just what he did to Mr. Jefford. But to the village too. And . . . and to Grandad. It's going to take ages for people to get over it."

Jamie didn't answer. He looked across the snowscape. For a while yet, it would stay here. And then it would be gone.

"We did do right, Jamie."

"Yes."

Not long now. They must head back towards the cottage. It was time.

Jamie turned his head. The church walls were still shrouded but, soon, they too would slowly re-emerge.

"What about the legend, Tim?"

"How d'you mean?"

"What d'you reckon now?"

Tim paused, as if uncertain. "Well, I suppose it's like Grandad said this morning. This power or whatever it is, it's not really under the stone or anything, it's more sort of inside people. It's *people* who—"

"D'you reckon he believes that?"

"I told you before. Believing things is his job."

"What about you? Do *you* believe it?"

"I . . . I think so. Well, I'm trying to. What about you?"

"I don't know really." Jamie shrugged. "I think he was right this time, anyway. As for next time—if there *is* a next time . . . well, perhaps I just sort of hope I'm not around to find out. Come on, we've got a train to catch."

And they ran, down through the snow. Their voices grew fainter. Then nothing was left but the tower, to watch them go.